Pascal Garnier was born in Paris in 1949. The prize-winning author of over sixty books, he remains a leading figure in contemporary French literature, in the tradition of Georges Simenon. He died in 2010.

Emily Boyce is an editor and in-house translator at Gallic Books. She lives in London.

'Wonderful ... Properly noir'
Ian Rankin

'Garnier plunges you into a bizarre, overheated world, seething death, writing, fictions and philosophy. He's a trippy, sleazy, sly and classy read'
A. L. Kennedy

'Horribly funny ... appalling and bracing in equal measure. Masterful'
John Banville

'Ennui, dislocation, alienation, estrangement – these are the colours on Garnier's palette. His books are out there on their own: short, jagged and exhilarating'
Stanley Donwood

'Garnier's world exists in the cracks and margins of ours; just off-key, often teetering on the surreal, yet all too plausible. His mordant literary edge makes these succinct novels stimulating and rewarding'
Sunday Times

'Deliciously dark ... painfully funny'
New York Times

'A mixture of Albert Camus and J. G. Ballard'
Financial Times

'A brilliant exercise in grim and gripping irony; makes you grin as well as wince'
Sunday Telegraph

'Bleak, often funny and never predictable'
The Observer

'A master of the surreal noir thriller – Luis Buñuel meets Georges Simenon'
Times Literary Supplement

'Small but perfectly formed darkest noir fiction told in spare, mordant prose ... Recounted with disconcerting matter-of-factness, Garnier's work is surreal and horrific in equal measure'
The Guardian

'A *jeu d'esprit* of hard-boiled symbolism, with echoes of Raymond Chandler, T. S. Eliot and the Marx Brothers'
Wall Street Journal

'Brief, brisk, ruthlessly entertaining ... Garnier makes bleakness pleasurable'
NPR

'Like Georges Simenon's books, Pascal Garnier's subversive, almost surreal tales come in slim little volumes, seldom more than 150 pages or so. But in that space he manages to say as much, and more memorably too, than many authors of books that are too heavy to hold'
Literary Review

'Superb'
The Spectator

'Deliciously sly and nuanced'
Irish Times

Also by Pascal Garnier:

Pascal Garnier: Gallic Noir Volumes 1, 2 and 3
The Panda Theory
The A26
Moon in a Dead Eye
The Front Seat Passenger
The Islanders
Boxes
Too Close to the Edge
The Eskimo Solution
Low Heights
C'est la Vie
A Long Way Off

Also available from Editions Gallic:

The Elegance of the Hedgehog by Muriel Barbery
The Vatican Cellars by André Gide
Clisson and Eugénie by Napoleon Bonaparte
The Gourmet by Muriel Barbery
The African by J. M. G. Le Clézio
I Remember by Georges Perec

How's the Pain?

How's the Pain?

Pascal Garnier

Translated from the French
by Emily Boyce

Introduction by John Banville

Gallic Books
London

A Gallic Book

First published in France as *Comment va la douleur?* by Zulma
Copyright © Zulma, 2006

English translation copyright © Gallic Books, 2012

Introduction © John Banville, 2020
The moral right of the author has been asserted

First published in Great Britain in 2012 by
Gallic Books, 59 Ebury Street, London, SW1W 0NZ
This edition published 2020

A CIP record for this book is available from the British Library

ISBN 9781910477922

Typeset in Fournier MT by Gallic Books

Printed in the UK by CPI
(CR0 4YY)

Introduction

If we are to describe Pascal Garnier as misanthropic, we shall have to invent another name for ordinary misanthropes. Garnier's deprecation of the world and the people who infest it is all-encompassing. He is as indignant as Jonathan Swift at the human state of affairs, only much funnier. His novels are at once bleak and hilarious, and his loathing of things in general is expressed with a peculiar insouciance – indeed, almost with gaiety.

He is often compared to Simenon, but while Simenon is stoically accepting of the *tragédie humaine*, Garnier is unrelentingly furious. He looks upon man and sees a ravening animal. Yet laughter will keep breaking in, and out.

How's the Pain? is one of the darkest of his works, and also one of the lightest. His skill in generating warmth out of a story centring on a mortally ill hit-man heading south to carry out his last commission is as mysterious as it is masterly.

Simon Marechall, the professional killer, is an old Africa hand, though the Africa he knew in his younger days is not the tawny, Edenic playground of Hemingway and Karen

Blixen — rather, it is Conrad's heart of darkness. For Simon was a mercenary, and one of his vividest memories is of shooting dead a fellow soldier of fortune who was wounded and begging to be put out of his misery.

How's the pain? The answer is *very bad indeed*. As one of his narrators puts it, 'Life leaves no survivors.'

Garnier was born in Paris in 1949 and died, of pancreatic cancer, in 2010. In a short autobiographical sketch, written at the behest of his French publishers, he confessed to having had

> a normal childhood in what you'd call the average French family — which felt more and more average the more it dawned on me that I'd been sold a world with no user's manual, lured in by false advertising.

When he was fifteen, he wrote, 'the state education system and I agreed to go our separate ways,' and thereafter he wandered for a decade through North Africa and the Middle and Far East. He returned to France, married, had a child, tried to get into rock and roll as a songwriter 'and landed with a resounding thud'. He divorced, married again, worked as a designer for women's magazines, and 'got up to the occasional bit of mischief'.

One would like to know a little more about just what kind of mischief it was he got up to. It seems clear that he was self-destructively familiar with the world of drink, drugs, sex and other potentially harmful pursuits.

With his early adventures behind him, he began to write fiction, the logical extension, as he saw it, of composing song lyrics. He published a collection of short stories, *L'année sabbatique*, after which 'another sixty-odd books were brought out . . . books for children [what *can* they be like?], books for adults, books labelled as noir or white, whatever – I've never been interested in that particular apartheid.'

The forces that rule in Garnier's universe are not consciously malign; it is just that, as in a Buster Keaton movie, things will insist on going wrong, with awful, comical inevitability. Nor is the mayhem relentless – in *How's the Pain?* especially, there are interludes of gentle reverie and even warmth.

As he pauses on his journey to the south, Simon encounters Bernard, a hapless young factory worker, and, a little later, a feral young woman named Fiona and her infant daughter, Violette. It is a measure of Garnier's achievement in this extraordinary novel that the little girl is one of the most striking characters among its small though vividly memorable cast. 'The only things she was interested in were her wiggly toes. When she could finally reach them, she would be a big girl.'

In *How's the Pain?*, as in all of Garnier's books, there is a great deal of violence, and the body count mounts steadily. The deaths, however, are not of great consequence, and occur almost incidentally. The true centre of the novel is the relationship between the irrepressibly optimistic Bernard and Simon the doomed killer – 'Without a father of his own, he had to find a substitute, and Monsieur Marechall fitted the bill.'

As the ill-matched quartet proceed on their journey to the south and Simon's final bit of lethal business, we seem to be accompanying them on a Sunday afternoon family outing:

> Violette agreed to be strapped in without protest, one eye open, the other shut, her lips pursed in resignation. Fiona joined Bernard in the front, which made him happy. Once he had put a bit of money aside, he would buy himself a car. Nothing as flashy as Monsieur Marechall's, but his own set of wheels all the same. He already had the child seat, which was a start.

It would be foolish to suggest that *How's the Pain?* offers an affirmative perspective on human affairs. It is as rancidly disenchanted as all of Garnier's work, and its author determinedly refuses, as always, to let us off the hook. Yet it is gloriously enjoyable both as an entertainment, and as a work of art. Garnier would probably scoff at the notion of himself as an artist, yet his achievement is an artistic one. The true and unflinching depiction of even the worst of what the world can do to its human inhabitants, so frail and fleeting, is never less than edifying, and surpassingly pleasurable. The pain is not always unbearable.

John Banville, 2020

Even a broken clock is right twice a day.
Proverb

The sound coming from somewhere in the darkness was barely audible, but it was enough to shatter his sleep. The drone of the moped grew louder until it was directly beneath his window, grating on his nerves like a dentist's drill boring into a decayed tooth. Then it faded into the distance, leaving nothing behind but a long rip through the fabric of the sleeping city. He hadn't opened his eyes or moved except to twitch his mouth in annoyance at the buzzing mechanical insect. Lying flat on his back with his hands crossed over his chest, Simon could have been a recumbent tomb effigy. One at a time he opened his heavy eyelids, gummed together like the rusty shutters of an old shop. He groped for his glasses on the bedside table, but could barely see any better once he had put them on. The pale light of dawn behind the floral-patterned lace curtains bathed the room in a uniform grey. Every object and item of furniture seemed devoid of substance, as if they had been hastily sketched on the walls. The bedspread, blanket and sheets had hardly been disturbed. He had slept peacefully, without waking. If that two-stroke engine had not roared in to break the spell, he would probably still have been asleep now. His travel clock beside the lamp showed 6.11 a.m. The alarm was set for seven. No matter, he was wide awake now. Besides, time did not follow its usual course in hotel rooms; it stagnated like the dead arm of a river.

Simon glanced around at his rudimentary universe: his shoes, sitting quietly at the foot of the bed, a sock rolled up inside each one; his jacket hanging limply over the back of the chair; the little table where he had emptied out the contents of his pockets, with the car keys and documents, his wallet, notebook, a pen, a handful of coins, a few banknotes and a large envelope addressed to Bernard Ferrand. He checked its contents: his Geneva bank account number and a power of attorney for Bernard, along with a short note saying, 'Thank you and good luck'. He gazed at it for a few moments, then screwed it up with a shrug and lobbed it into the wastepaper basket. Next to the envelope sat an apple and a skipping rope, still in its colourful plastic wrapping. A poor copy of Van Gogh's *Sunflowers* hung on the olive-green wall. The bathroom light was still on. A notice on the back of the door informed guests of the fire drill, room rates, mealtimes and so on.

Was it him that creaked or the bed, as he extricated himself from the sheets? He rubbed his neck. Wretched trapped nerves. His knees were like banister knobs. His calves were dry and hairy like crab claws, his toenails hard as ancient ivory, like the claws of an aged dog. He yawned, got up and raised a corner of the curtain. The same pallid light outside as in. The clouds were low, clinging like tufts of cotton wool to the mountains encircling Vals-les-Bains, Ucel and Saint-Julien-du-Serre. It was impossible to tell what lay beyond. Between the streaks of rain running down the window, he could just about make out the muddy waters of the Volane flowing past the Béatrix-spring rotunda.

'It was too good to last. The forecast says it's going to carry on raining all week.'

'You're the one who wanted to take the waters. We'll just have to go to the pictures.'

This was a conversation Simon had overheard the previous evening, from the neighbouring table in the hotel restaurant. A retired couple: the wife shaking her head over the menu, the husband hiding behind *Le Dauphiné*. The front page was taken up with the news of the death of a well-known film producer, pictured sporting a dazzling display of dentures and a glitzy starlet on each arm.

Simon tucked into his Vichyssoise and fillets of sole and saved the apple for later, which is to say, now. He bit into it. A little floury. Disappointed, he put it down and went into the bathroom.

He had still not worked out the shower. It was a toss-up between freezing-cold or boiling-hot water. Perhaps because his body sensed that it had already been deserted, it refused to respond to his brain's orders. The glass tumbler slipped from his hands and smashed on the tiled floor. He knocked his elbow, banged his knee and cut himself shaving. All he saw in the mirror now was the outline of a blurred face seeking anonymity. A dab of aftershave and that was it, done. He changed his underwear out of respect for the people who would soon be dealing with his corpse.

Once dressed, he paced the few steps from the window to the bed, from the bed back to the window. Then he took the skipping rope out of its packaging. The brightly coloured box showed a little girl in a pink dress playing in a daisy-strewn meadow. He had bought it the day before in the souvenir shop next to the hotel, just before it closed. The shop assistant had smiled at her last, curious sale of the day. The rope was white, with red handles. He tested its strength by tugging on it sharply. 'Made in China', he read with suspicion. Then he placed the chair underneath the frosted-glass ceiling light with its stylised tulips, and clambered onto it. He carefully tied one end of the rope around the hook on the ceiling and looped the other around his neck. He was perfectly calm. He was not quite sure what to do with his hands. He clasped them behind his back and waited, wearily watching the raindrops streaking down the windowpane.

Maybe it was sleeping too long beside his mother's cold body, or else it was the permanently damp atmosphere that had made Bernard feel so out of sorts – stiff, sniffling, fuzzy-headed. What was it with these old folk, loading their dirty work onto him as if he were some mule? It was a good thing Fiona and Violette had stayed put. Still, hey ho, better get on with the job.

The lift took Bernard up to the fourth floor. The doors opened and a bell pinged. The corridor was empty. His footsteps were muffled by the brown, leaf-patterned carpet which seemed to go on for ever. 401, 402, 403 ... He sneezed and then blew his nose as quietly as he could. 404, 405, 406. He was a couple of minutes early. Monsieur Marechall was a stickler for punctuality. He waited. Water dripped off his cagoule onto his shoes. Eight o'clock on the dot. Very gently, he turned the handle of the door which opened without the slightest creak. Just as planned, Monsieur Marechall was standing on the chair, facing the window, hands behind his back like a naughty schoolboy made to stand in the corner. He hadn't flinched, though he knew Bernard had come in. Took guts.

Apart from a ripple along the curtain folds, nothing moved. It was like looking at a photograph. Snatches of conversation from the road outside, a shrill laugh, a car door slamming, an engine starting up. The last sound jolted Bernard into action. Two steps forward. He closed his eyes and kicked the chair from under Monsieur Marechall's feet. A cracking sound but no cry, just the crash of the chair on the floor and a whoosh of displaced air. Bernard remembered a wooden puppet he had had when he was little; you pulled a string and its arms and legs jigged about. He waited until all he could hear was a rhythmic creaking that grew softer and softer before he opened one eye. One of Simon's shoes had fallen off, an expensive loafer deformed by a bunion. Bernard did not dare look up. He collected the cash, keys and car documents from the table, along with the envelope, as agreed. He was hungry and bit into the half-eaten apple. Tasteless. It was hard to find a decent apple these days. He sneezed again. They were saying it would rain all week. He left the room and shut the door behind him. No point saying goodbye to a dead man. At the end of the corridor, Bernard found the lift in use. He took the stairs.

They had met a few days earlier on a park bench beside the Volane, opposite the casino. It was a Saturday, some time around 11 a.m. A bravely struggling sun made the landscape look like a naïve painting. The trees were green, the flowers pink, yellow and red, the sky blue and the shadows grey. The pathways were teeming with people, as wedding parties gathered at the foot of the grand stone steps – the perfect spot to line up the families in front of the camera. It was a little bit like paradise, with everyone dressed up, perfumed and polished like the best china, all kissing each other or crying with happiness.

'Could you all move in a bit please? And a bit more? The lady with the blue hat, could you take a step back? Thanks, that's great! Now just the bride and groom please, among the roses.'

The photographer was a true professional; he had no qualms about destroying the flowerbeds or tyrannising his models to ensure that this would truly be the most beautiful day of their lives.

'Get down on bended knee please, sir – that's it, like Prince Charming. Smile, smile! Take his hand ... Perfect!'

The fixed grimaces on the newlyweds' faces suggested either they desperately needed to pee or their new shoes were rubbing. The groom's suit looked stiff as a board, while his bride stood surrounded by masses of netting that could have been spun from a candyfloss machine. Clinging to the train like limpets, the bridesmaids twisted their ankles tottering in their first pair of heels. Mothers dabbed their eyes, fathers puffed out their chests with pride, kids played catch, sending up eddies of dust. Groups of spa visitors, recognisable from the cups in wicker holders dangling from straps slung over their shoulders, mingled with the families and took pictures, condescending to share in the simple rituals of the indigenous population.

'Isn't this lovely?'

'You think so?'

'Well, yes. Seeing all these people so happy, it's nice, isn't it?'

'How do you know they're happy?'

'You can tell.'

'You can't trust appearances. It's usually all for show. What about you, are you happy?'

'Depends ... yes, I think so.'

'Are you married?'

'No.'

'What happened to your hand?'

'An accident at work. One of the machines. Lost two fingers.'

'Nasty.'

'It hurts a bit, but it's only my little finger and fourth finger. I never used them. Plus it's my left hand and I'm right-handed.'

'Well, that's all right then. You just lost a bit of weight.'

'It was my fault. I'd had a bit to drink. I didn't use the safety guard. But my boss is a good guy and he's taking me back, in a different job ... The pay's not so good, but at least it's work. I've been lucky!'

'A real stroke of luck, I'm sure! Let me introduce myself. I'm Simon Marechall.'

'Bernard Ferrand. Are you here for the spa?'

'Are you joking? Do I look like one of those decrepit old crocks?' Simon asked, horrified. 'Just look at them with those ridiculous sunhats, the silly cups round their necks, their baggy shorts and knock-knees. Their bandy legs are like battered Louis XV chairs: it's an antiques market! They should have dust covers put over them. No, no,' he concluded, 'I'm just passing through. What about you?'

'Um, just passing through too, while my hand heals. My mother lives in Vals. We don't see each other very often so I thought I'd make the most of my time off.'

'So there are people who really live here. I thought they must be film extras. You know the area then?'

'Not very well. I live in Bron, near Lyon. I'm not from here; I just come now and then to see my mother.'

'Is there much to do?'

'There's the casino. You can go for walks, visit the Château de Cros, see the volcanic rocks. Then there's Jean Ferrat, of course.'

'Jean Ferrat, the singer?'

'Yes, he's from Antraigues. Sometimes you see him at the market on Sunday mornings.'

'That's terrific!'

'You like Jean Ferrat then?'

'Very much. Do you?'

'Not specially.'

'Bit before your time, I expect.'

'It's more that I've heard my mother singing his songs so often, it's almost like he's a friend of the family.'

Laughing, Simon took a tissue out of his pocket to wipe his sunglasses. He had grey eyes, the colour of steel: cold and hard.

'I like you very much, young man. How old are you?'

'I'll be twenty-two next month.'

'How would you like to have lunch with me?'

'I can't, I have to go back to my mother's. I'm already late and I need to pick up some bread.'

'What a shame. How about this evening?'

'Um, OK.'

'Do you know of any good restaurants?'

'Chez Mireille is supposed to be good. I think it's a bit pricey but ...'

'Don't worry about that, it'll be my treat. Tonight at seven thirty then. Come and meet me at the Grand Hôtel de Lyon. Simon Marechall, room 406.'

'OK then, thanks.'

Simon's hand was cold, dry and tense. With his black shades back on, Simon seemed to Bernard like the night glaring down, though in fact the older man was slightly shorter than him. One set off towards the hotel district, the other in the direction of the old town.

Even though the street was bathed in sunlight, Madame Ferrand's little shop remained hopelessly gloomy. It was years since she had pulled back the faded cretonne curtain across the shop window, and its dust-coated folds made it impossible for passers-by to see in. But it didn't matter, since nothing was for sale here any more. It had become Madame Ferrand's apartment. The back room was used as a kitchen-cum-bathroom and a small adjoining storeroom served as a bedroom. The 'shop' itself, as Madame Ferrand still called it, now formed the living room. It was furnished with a sagging sofa heaped with cushions, throws and blankets of dubious cleanliness; three ill-assorted chairs; a wobbly pedestal table; a dining table with flaking varnish, and a curious floor lamp in the shape of a life-sized nude Negress, wearing a raffia lampshade askew on her head. The floor was covered with a patchwork of threadbare rugs. On the walls, dog-eared adverts for long-gone brands, posters of dead singers, and tourist-office promotions for countries since ravaged by war bandaged the wounds in the peeling wallpaper. Odd remnants of shelving, racks and spotlights bore witness to the owner's many and various ventures, snuffed out one by one by stubbornly adverse fate.

Madame Ferrand had invested the sum total of her meagre savings in these modest premises twenty years earlier. She had had no hesitation in entrusting little Bernard, then aged two, to the care of her parents, leaving her free to seek her fortune in Vals-les-Bains. Why Vals-les-Bains? Perhaps because of Jean Ferrat, whose revolutionary lyrics could not fail to ignite the pure working-class heart of a mother seduced by a stockbroker from Lyon, who vanished without trace when baby Bernard was born. Unless it was something as mundane as an ad in *Le Dauphiné* that put the idea into her head one lonely evening, kindling in her the hope of escaping her unremittingly squalid fate.

She was thirty-five, feisty, determined, good with her hands and not without talent. Ignoring the derision of neighbouring shopkeepers, she worked on her hats by night and fixed the place up during the day, successfully transforming an old-fashioned haberdasher's into a stylish millinery boutique in the space of a month. Chez Anaïs opened on schedule at the end of May, just in time for the tourist season. But by October, she had to face facts: she had not found her clientele. Her extravagant headpieces certainly amused the spa visitors who came to try them on, giggling in front of the mirrors, but they never bought anything.

27

After a period of understandable despondency, she sold her stock to a ragman for next to nothing and, with the same enthusiasm and pugnacity as before, opened a local handicrafts shop with a young hippy by the name of Daphne. A new sign, 'Aux Herbes Tendres', went up in place of the old. They sold beeswax candles, real leather belts and bags, brass jewellery, weird preserves, strange infusions and incense sticks, a lot of incense sticks, some of which were kept tucked inside Daphne's long woollen coat. Business was going pretty well until the day Anaïs's partner ran off with the till, leaving her with nothing but her eyes to cry with, a few armfuls of lavender and bitter memories of her first Sapphic love affair. '*La femme est l'avenir de l'homme*,' crooned Jean Ferrat, so couldn't a woman be another woman's future too? She was furious with Jean Ferrat that autumn and furious with the rest of humanity too, which is what set her thinking about going into dog grooming. You rarely come across a retired couple on a spa break without one of those hideous golden poodles in tow. Of course, Anaïs knew nothing about dogs and the equipment costs would be substantial, but nothing ventured, nothing gained. This time, she was sure she was onto something. She'd had it with the human race and was putting her faith in man's best friend. Come spring, Madame Ferrand donned an immaculate white coat to welcome the first customers to her pooch parlour. But at the beginning of July, she was forced to close the doors due to an unfortunate incident. A faulty switch on a drier had turned a dachshund called Caruso into a hot dog. The sale of the equipment just about covered the legal fees.

Anaïs was by no means the only one to experience a run of bad luck. One by one, the shops along Rue Jean-Jaurès went under, turning it into a ghost town. Only those supplying life's basic essentials (namely the baker, the butcher and the tobacconist) were able to survive. This part of town, where tourists wandered aimlessly as if roaming the ruins of a lost civilisation, seemed destined for oblivion. After buying a few postcards, they would hurry back across the Volane to the reassuring shade of manicured hotel gardens.

But Anaïs was not one to throw in the towel at the first hurdle, nor the second, nor even the third. There must be a lesson to be learnt from this string of failures. One evening, as she groped for her glasses in the storeroom, her light-bulb moment came: 'That's it! Seeing!' The scent of incense wafted back to her as she recalled her former partner's mysterious revelations, secrets she had made her solemnly swear never to share.

'No way am I going to keep that to myself, you old bitch!'

True, she might have drunk a little too much rum from the bottle of Negrita she was clutching, but she was just as shrewd as the next person!

Within a month she had digested the Egyptian Book of the Dead, that of the Tibetans and even the Popol Vuh. She mastered palm reading as easily as a shareholder learning about the stock exchange or a racegoer studying form. Finally, she saw a future ahead. Even better, the investment required was paltry: a pedestal table, a tarot set, a clock and that was it. Not to mention the fact that, in order for her to concentrate, she would need to be in complete darkness, drastically reducing her electricity bills. With the last of her money she had business cards printed to drop through letterboxes. It was cold, it was winter, she wheezed and her legs puffed up, but the Negrita kept her going. All she needed to do was wait.

Her first three clients suffered violent deaths in quick succession. One choked on a plum stone, another was hit head-on by a bus on her way to mass and the last was devoured by her own dog. Rumours spread quickly in small towns like this and nobody else took the risk of consulting her.

Anaïs took to coughing to pass the time, a hacking cough which tolled like a death knell inside her chest and which she had come to accept, like an old dog that had latched onto her.

In one last, admirable burst of optimism, she wrote a slate sign: 'Anaïs's Bric-à-Brac', which she hung in the shop window. The only remnants of her failed ventures were a few musty felt hats, some bunches of dried flowers, three or four candles which had lost their scent, a dozen cracked leather dog collars and a tarot set. Strangely enough, she sold the lot.

These days she lived off her incurable cough, which brought her a small disability allowance, along with the modest but regular parcels she received from Bernard. It was enough to buy her daily bottle of Negrita, enabling her to watch calmly as the dust settled like grey snow on a life that should not have been. 'My past is a joke, my present's a disaster, thank goodness I have no future,' she would say to console herself.

'Mother, lunch is almost ready, come and sit down!'

Walking past Béatrix ice-cream parlour down the road from his hotel, Simon gave in to a childish whim. He sat down at a table underneath the plane trees whose leaves filtered the sunlight, casting extraordinary shadows. With the defiance of a little boy, he ordered the biggest and most expensive ice cream on the menu. While he waited for it to arrive, he flicked through the spa brochure he had picked up from reception that morning. The town boasted six springs: Constantine was the best for treating weight problems, dyspepsia and gout; Précieuse was the one to go to for liver conditions and diabetes; Dominique was very effective against anaemia and fatigue; Désirée was recommended for its laxative effects; Rigolette was prescribed for colitis; Camuse, to ease digestion. These waters could only be drunk on prescription, but there were three others – Saint-Jean, Favorite and Béatrix – which could be consumed in limitless quantities. The list of the conditions they were capable of curing was both endless and disconcerting: industrial dermatitis, nasal fractures, tropical liver diseases, trigger finger, abnormally large intestines ... There were as many ailments to treat as there were ice creams on the menu. Who could claim not to suffer from a single one of them?

He glanced up. The average age of the clientele was somewhere between sixty and a hundred. Though he fell into this age bracket himself, the sight of so many pensioners in one place made him dizzy. While he had always considered his presence on earth to be a miscasting and had done his best to distance himself from his playmates from a tender age, he had never felt so trapped, in the clutches of some merciless predator. A young waitress set down in front of him the huge glass of garish ice cream studded with ridiculous cocktail umbrellas. Aside from her, he could see only three humanoids who had so far escaped the ravages of time. All of them were on wheels (bicycle, skateboard and rollerblades) as they zipped past, intent on dodging the Zimmer frames.

Why on earth had he stopped at Vals-les-Bains? It was simply down to a pun. A Strauss waltz had been playing on France Musique as he drove towards the town. 'A last waltz ... a last Vals?' Admittedly a violent bout of sickness had also forced him to stop for an hour, leaving him feeling shaky. He was in luck, a Belgian couple had just cancelled and there was one room left at the Grand Hôtel de Lyon. He had planned to stay just one night, but when he woke up to a glimpse of spring sunshine, a coffee and some excellent croissants, something in the air had made him want to truant for the day.

He still hadn't touched his ice cream, which was beginning to resemble a jaundiced cowpat. He toyed with his spoon, looking at his reflection in its curved surfaces. What had come over him, inviting that lad to dinner? He probably took him for an old queer. What if he didn't turn up? He hadn't seemed too bright, but that was what he liked about him: his honesty, his awkwardness, and that bandaged hand he moved about like a glove puppet. There was no denying it, he had made some strange choices since his arrival, like this ice cream he had never even wanted in the first place and which was now just a mess. He tried a mouthful anyway. All the flavours had mingled together and it was impossible to identify a single one. It was just cold and sweet.

While he was fishing for change in his jacket pocket, his revolver almost fell out.

'Shit, it really is time to call it a day.'

'So why's this man invited you to dinner then? You don't think he might be a poofter?'

'Don't think so, no. He seems normal.'

'What's "normal"? Everyone seems normal, but they're not really. Anyway, you're a big boy now, you can look after yourself.'

'Don't you want any more of your chop, Mother?'

'No, it's too fatty.'

'Lamb's always a bit fatty, that's what makes it so tasty. You never eat anything.'

'Well, you can't do everything. Eat or drink, you have to make a choice.'

'You drink too much. You smoke too much as well. No wonder you're always tired.'

'I like being tired, it's relaxing. What are you doing today?'

'Not sure. It's a nice day, might go for a walk down by the river. How about I make you some vegetable soup for tonight?

You like veggie soup, don't you?'

'If you like. How's your hand?'

'It's all right. I went to see Dr Garcin this morning to get the dressing changed. He asked after you.'

'And what did you say?'

'That you were fine.'

'You're a rotten liar ... just as well.'

'And what are you going to do?'

'Same as usual. A nice nap before I go to bed.'

It was a place only he knew. You went under the bridge before taking a pebbly path beside the Volane for about fifteen minutes. Then you had to jump from rock to rock, without worrying about getting your feet wet, to reach a little sandy cove shaded by gnarled willows. No one could see you. The bubbling of the water drowned out the hubbub of the town and the cars on the road above. He had discovered this spot when on holiday here at the age of ten. It was in the days when his mother was selling strange herbs with Daphne. He'd never much liked that lady. Firstly, she was ugly, with all that red hair and hippy clothes. She couldn't smile properly either; every time she tried, stroking his head, she looked like the wicked stepmother offering Snow White the poisoned apple. She smelt bad and painted her nails black like claws. If he'd been a dog, he would have bitten her.

Bernard leant against the warm rock, took off his shoes and socks and wiggled his toes in the grey sand. The pebbles formed a pool where the water could catch its breath before continuing along its course, foaming at the mouth. Dragonflies flitted across the surface and sometimes you might see a trout circling in the clear water below. They were beautiful, the dragonflies, as delicate and glittery as Tinkerbell. The trout were pretty too; so gentle, so shiny, so alive. Once he had caught one in his hand. That was a moment he would never forget. It was like holding life itself between his fingers with its golden eyes, supple body, shimmering scales and gills that pulsed like pipe valves. He stroked it for a long time, too long. It bucked one last time and all that was left in his hands was a limp, motionless object. He had tried to put it back in the water but it had instantly capsized, baring its white belly to the sky. He had buried it tearfully, right there under the willow stump. Even after washing his hands ten times, it took two days to get rid of the smell of sludge. He never did it again.

No, this Monsieur Simon Marechall was no queer. He had invited him out because he liked him, simple as that. It was spending all her time shut away in that dump of a shop that made his mother see the dark side of everything. Anyway, he had known queers who were no worse than the people who didn't like queers. All you had to do was say no. Once he had said yes, just to see what would happen. It was in the third year of secondary school and the boy's surname was Gambin or Gamblin or something. Gamblin's dick had the same effect on him as the trout between his hands. He let it go. Gamblin wanted to be a diver when he grew up. He swam like a fish. Everyone dreamt of being something then: diver, pilot, fireman or farmer. But Bernard had never found his calling.

'What do you want to do for a living?'

'Dunno.'

Having miraculously got to the end of the fourth year, borne along like a stowaway, he was advised to take the vocational route, not being academically inclined. Baking, hairdressing, mechanics, plumbing – he was happy to have a go at anything, only nothing went right. However hard he tried, however much he concentrated, nothing went in. Sometimes he thought he had understood, but he was so used to being taken for an idiot that when things seemed too straightforward, he undid everything he had done and it would all go to pot. It was only during his military service that he finally achieved something, passing his driving test first time. It was the best day of his life – well, not the whole day. That night, after celebrating with some mates, he had gone joy-riding in a Jeep and ended up inside for two weeks. It was still a good memory though. The best. In truth, he had no other memories to speak of, just little things like the trout, Gamblin's dick, random bits and pieces that resurfaced now and then for him to toy with in his head, the way a baby plays with its feet. Mostly, though, each day just wiped out the day before.

A fly landed on his knee. It was young and quivering with energy. In a fraction of a second, Bernard held it captive under his hand. He could feel it batting around inside. It tickled. Slowly he spread his fingers and the insect zigzagged away. When it came to catching flies, he was unbeatable. Shame you couldn't make a career out of it.

He stood up and looked for a really flat pebble. Skimming

stones was another of his talents. The pebble glanced across the surface of the water like a flying saucer, bouncing six times before reaching the opposite bank. It was a hot day. He took his clothes off and lay in the current, holding his injured hand up towards the sky like a periscope so as not to get the bandage wet. He wasn't thinking about anything now. It was just nice to dissolve into the water.

Leaning back in his chair with his head tilted back, Simon smoked a cigarette and watched Bernard tucking into his daube of beef, his nose almost in his plate. It was a fascinating sight. The young man used his fork like a dagger, stabbing it into the meat to hold it in place. Then he cut off big chunks which vanished into his mouth with mechanical regularity. As he swallowed each barely chewed mouthful, his throat and shoulders shuddered slightly before he began all over again, taking the occasional glug of water to wash it down.

'You've got quite an appetite!'

'I always do. I'll eat anything – and the food here's damned good, isn't it?'

'It is very good, yes.'

In no time at all, the plate was wiped clean, sparkling as if it had just come out of the dishwasher.

'Aren't you going to finish yours, Monsieur Marechall?'

'Help yourself!'

'I could eat beef stew out of a bin.'

Chez Mireille was one of those bijou restaurants found in all small provincial towns. The walls were painted blue and pink, with intricate gilt patterns to give a touch of class. For passers-by peering in, the cosy scene was framed by lacy curtains with satin tiebacks. Mireille, a busty blonde of a certain age, glided seamlessly from table to table checking that everything was to her customers' liking. She was like the little dancer inside a music box, spinning in time to the tinkling of a Mozart tune.

Just like the wedding parties in Parc Saint-Jean that morning, everybody in the room was clean, attractive and pleasant. They spoke little and quietly. A dropped teaspoon caused quite a stir. Here, too, the average age veered towards the top of the scale; Bernard was the odd one out. He had dressed for the occasion, which is to say he had swapped his sloppy tracksuit for a pastel shirt, a navy-blue jacket that was slightly too short in the sleeve and a pair of dark-grey trousers. He could not believe his luck, and sat beaming at everyone and everything – even the water jug and bread basket. He had passed Chez Mireille countless times but never dreamt of going in. Now here he was lapping up every second and it was a pleasure to see. Pushing away the second plate as spotless as the first, he leant back in his chair with a satisfied sigh. Watching him, Simon was riveted.

'Cigarette?'

'No, I don't smoke.'

'And you don't drink wine either?'

'No. It makes my head spin, I don't like it.'

'Very sensible. Now tell me, what did your job involve?'

'We made clamps.'

'What for?'

'I dunno, just clamps. Big ones, small ones, medium ones. You had to make a certain number in an hour and then they got packed up and sent who knows where.'

'Wasn't that rather repetitive?'

'It's a job. Once you know what you're doing it's just mindless. Pretty cushy really. What about you, what do you do?'

'Pest control. Getting rid of rats, mice, pigeons, fleas, cockroaches, that sort of thing.'

'Is it going well?'

'Very. But I'm getting on a bit. I'm thinking of selling up and retiring.'

'Lucky you, retiring! Doesn't suit everyone though. There was this old guy at the factory and for his retirement present we got him this beautiful spinning rod. He never stopped going on about all the fishing trips he was planning when he stopped work. Two weeks later, what did he do? Threw himself into the river. As for me ... well, I wish I was retired already.'

'And what would you do if you were?'

'Nothing.'

'Don't you have any interests? You wouldn't want to travel?'

'No. I'd just like to have enough money to do nothing.'

'You'd get bored.'

'I don't think I would. When you're out of work and broke,

you're bored because you spend the whole time thinking about how you're going to get some money. But if you've already got it, doing nothing's easy.'

'Don't you like reading or going to the cinema?'

'I've got a problem with books. When I get to the bottom of the page, I can't remember the beginning, so it takes me ages to get through them. And I fall asleep in the dark at the cinema. So what are you going to do when you retire?'

'I don't know. I like the sea. And boats.'

Mireille brought over the cheese trolley. Bernard took a wedge of everything. Simon ordered another bottle of Cornas.

'Can you believe how many cheeses they've got? It's insane. I haven't even heard of half of them. Is that all you're having, Monsieur Marechall?'

'I had some Gruyère.'

'You're just like my mother, you eat out of your glass. So you're into boats, are you? Model ones or ones you go on?'

'Ones you go on, as you put it.'

'And where would you go, on your boat?'

'Anywhere. The best bit is setting sail.'

'I'm the opposite – the best bit for me would be getting there. So you've been on a lot of boats then?'

'I've travelled a fair amount. What I'd like is just to sail from island to island, without following a plan.'

'Nice are they, islands?'

'Some of them are lovely, yes. In fact each one has its own charm, even the bleakest.'

'Don't you end up going round and round in circles?'

'No more than anywhere else on earth. If you think about it, our planet is nothing more than an island in space.'

'Maybe, but a pretty big one. It'd take quite a while to get around the whole thing.'

'Not all that long. Anyway once you've had enough of an island, you just set sail again and it's like starting from scratch.'

'Why would you want to start from scratch? You seem like you've done well in life. I can't seem to get off the starting line.'

Probably by association, Bernard ordered the floating island for dessert. Simon was happy just to finish off the bottle of wine. He could consume huge quantities without showing the slightest sign of inebriation; only his gaze became more intense and unsettling. He never stumbled or raised his voice. In actual fact, he couldn't stand drunks. He generally stuck to water, so as to keep a steady hand. But some days, some nights ... The strange thing about this young blockhead was that he wasn't actually stupid. He displayed a kind of guileless common sense which Simon found refreshing. It reminded him of the possibility of a simpler life. It was like coming across a spring gushing with cool water at the end of a long hot walk. Bernard's vulnerability made him invincible.

They left the restaurant and headed back up Rue Jean-Jaurès (steering clear of Bernard's mother's shop), crossed the Volane and walked down Boulevard de Vernon towards the Grand Hôtel de Lyon. It was a mild evening, almost as bright as daylight with the full moon swinging like a pendulum amid the stars. They passed only two people on their way: a man walking his dog and another leaning against the trunk of a plane tree, vomiting.

'Which countries have you been to, Monsieur Marechall?'

'Oh, I've been all over the place: Asia, the Middle East, Africa, Latin America, anywhere that's had a war. I was in the army before setting up my business.'

'Ah, I see. Being in the army takes you places. I was in Germany once; even then it was just over the border. Apart from the language it's the same as here. I went to Switzerland with school once too. It was really nice, just like the postcards. Have you been?'

'Yes. It's very pretty. It makes you want to die.'

'Why do you say that?'

'Well, because it's so quiet ... and full of flowers.'

'You're right actually. They know a whole lot about geraniums.'

'So what's this building here?'

'That's the Vals mineral water plant.'

There was something feudal about this massive structure whose shadow loomed over half the street. Its arched windows reflected the moon's pearly light. Most of the surrounding warehouses had been boarded up, making the building's long, towering walls seem even more formidable. Who could tell what dark deeds went on behind closed doors? Simon seemed entranced.

'It's like the hull of the *Queen Mary* coming in to dock ...' he muttered.

'That's a boat, isn't it? What was it called again?'

'It's more than a boat. It's a giant of the seas!'

'Only here, the water's inside rather than all around it. Thirty million bottles come out of there every year. The factory's been going over a hundred years, so that's a whole lot of water – enough to make the place float!'

'You're right. Perhaps it will sail away one day.'

'I was only joking.'

'Have you been to the sea much, Bernard?'

'No, never. The closest thing I've seen to the sea is Lake Geneva.'

'Would you like to go?'

'Yes, why not?'

They carried on walking in silence, Bernard trying to imagine a body of water greater than Lake Geneva, Simon racking his brains to think of the ultimate island.

The multicoloured lights strung among the trees outside Béatrix ice-cream parlour were still on. A waiter in shirtsleeves was clearing tables and stacking chairs. A few stragglers hung around the rotunda hoping for some excitement before returning to their hotel rooms to stuff themselves with sleeping pills. The more optimistic ones made straight for the casino whose lights could be seen flickering through the trees. It was only ten thirty, and Simon wasn't ready to go to bed.

'One last drink?'

'No, I'd better get going. I have to look after my mother. Thanks again for dinner, I really enjoyed it.'

'OK then. See you around.'

'Tomorrow's market day.'

'I'll see you there then. Good night.'

Simon ordered a pear brandy in the lounge. Two men were playing snooker, badly, but they strutted around like world champions. While waiting for his drink Simon inspected the bookshelves and lighted on an old, yellowed copy of *Treasure Island*. He settled into a cracked leather armchair and thumbed through it, hoping to recapture the pleasure he had felt when he first read it. The island had not changed, but he had.

Anaïs was snoring loudly on the sofa, a spirituality guide propped open on her chest like a little tent. The blanket had slid off and her dress had ridden up, revealing her legs splayed wide. She wasn't wearing any knickers. Her bushy pubic hair crept up over her belly. Bernard saw nothing indecent in the scene; he was just a bit surprised that that was where he came from. He put the book down, taking care to mark her page, before lifting his mother up and putting her to bed. He tucked her in, pulled the quilt up to her chin and planted a kiss on her forehead. She rolled over with a moan.

On market days, Rue Jean-Jaurès was unrecognisable. The stalls lining the pavements hid the empty windows of closed-down shops. A constant stream of people swarmed down the narrow street, their heaped baskets occasionally colliding and creating pedestrian traffic jams. The cool morning air fragrant with the smells of flowers, fruit, roast chicken and fresh fish could tempt even the most abstemious to indulge. Trestle tables sagged under the weight of mountains of cherries, transformed by sunlight into piles of shimmering rubies. Simon couldn't resist buying himself a handful, biting into them as he walked. There were no subtle shades here, only vivid kaleidoscope colours.

Market traders improvised skits to charm customers into parting with their cash. In front of a stall selling local handicrafts in the shape of goatskin drums, snake-head charms, plywood Bantu masks, glass-bead necklaces, elephants made out of tyres and an array of boiled leather hats, a German tourist was haggling over a bag that appeared to be made from reptile skin. The seller was a burly African wearing a thick overcoat despite the heat.

'*Nein! Moi acheter, mais pas vrai croco!*'

'*Si! Croco véritable!*'

'*Si croco véritable, moi pas acheter. Imitation, oui.*'

The vendor rolled his eyes, but since neither of them had much grasp of the language the transaction soon descended into farce. The poor man's prospective customer was a hardline eco-warrior, signalled by her tow-coloured hair cut in a severe bob and Birkenstock sandals. From the way she was clutching it to her chest, it was obvious she liked the bag, but the idea that it might have come from a living creature repulsed her. Still, the consummate salesman would not back down.

'*Vrai croco!* My uncle kill it with his hands! Good price for you!'

'*Nein!* Plastic, yes, animal killed, no.'

It was all getting too confusing. The trader wearily agreed to knock the price down, reluctantly admitting that the bag was indeed made of plastic, 'but good plastic!' The German woman left delighted with her purchase while the stallholder counted the banknotes, making a gesture to indicate that she must have a screw loose.

Further up, where the road opened out in front of the post office, two trucks stacked with tapes and CDs vied noisily with each other, belching out the voices of dead or obscure singers, accordion music, Algerian raï tunes, rock and local folk in a primordial cacophony. Other vehicles spewed hunting gear from their open flanks; everything from thick hand-knitted socks to deerstalkers, long johns, tartan shirts, sheepskin-lined gilets and the full range of combat trousers.

There were garments to tempt the ladies, too. Almost inconceivably large flesh-coloured knickers and bras hung from metal hoops, swaying among flirtily floral nylon blouses and other items from an era so remote that it was difficult to imagine any survivors still out shopping.

In front of one of these stalls, Simon felt a hand on his shoulder.

'Hello, Monsieur Marechall.'

'Hello, Bernard.'

'So, what do you think?'

'It's very ... colourful.'

'Ooh, look over there!'

'What?'

'The tall man with the white hair and the moustache!'

Simon's eyes followed the direction of Bernard's finger. A dignified old man in an olive-green velvet suit was filling a crate with vegetables.

'Yes?'

'It's Jean Ferrat!'

'Good heavens, you're right, it looks just like him.'

'It doesn't just look like him, it is him! You're in luck, he doesn't come every Sunday.'

'Very lucky, indeed. Now, Bernard, do you have time for a coffee?'

'Yes, I've done my shopping.'

Nobody was asking Jean Ferrat for his autograph.

They sat outside the betting café facing the church and ordered two espressos. The smell of pastis and cigarette smoke wafted out from the doorway along with the shouts of punters clustered like flies around the TV screen. Simon insisted on moving to a table where he could sit with his back to the wall, even though it meant being out of the shade of an umbrella advertising some brand of aperitif.

'You did the same thing at the restaurant last night.'

'It's a habit of mine.'

Bernard looked around smiling, his shopping basket wedged between his knees. The comings and goings of the motley crowd seemed to delight him.

'I love market days. There's a sort of holiday atmosphere. There's no one along here during the week. Apparently it was a bit livelier before.'

'Before what?'

'Before the factories shut. The pulp mills, basalt ... there were jobs, you know. Now the only places where there's any life are the spas, the hotels and casino – and that's only in high season.'

'I think I smell roast chicken, do you?'

'Oh, that's me, I bought one. My mother doesn't eat much but the smell of roast chicken always gets her mouth watering. She'll only have a wing, but it's something at least. I'll make some mash to go with it.'

'You love your mother very much, don't you?'

50

'Of course, she's my mother. Everyone loves their own mother.'

'But from what you've told me, she hasn't had a great deal of time for you over the years.'

'I don't blame her for that. She just wanted to make a success of things. If everything had gone to plan, she would have sent for me.'

'And how does she manage when you're not around?'

'A couple of neighbours pop in ... I send her a bit of money. It'll be harder now though; I won't be earning as much.'

'Would you like some cherries?'

'Yes, thanks. They're still expensive – this is my first of the season. I should make a wish.'

The sweetness took away the bitter taste of the coffee. Bernard puffed out his cheeks and spat out the stone which bounced off a 'No Entry' sign on the other side of the road.

'You've got a good aim.'

'I was catapult champion when I was a kid.'

'What did you wish for?' asked Simon.

'If you say it out loud, it won't come true.'

Simon lit a cigarette. The smoke coming out of his nostrils made him look like a dragon. Bernard was tying knots in the cherry stalks.

'Tell me, Bernard, do you have a driving licence?'

'Damn right I do! I passed first time when I was in the army.'

'Are you by any chance free for a couple of days?'

'To do what?'

'I have to get to Cap d'Agde for a business trip but I'm

feeling rather tired. I could really use a driver. Three hundred euros a day, all expenses paid. Only we'd need to leave early tomorrow morning. How does that sound?'

'Are you saying it would be six hundred euros for two days?'

'Exactly.'

'Jesus! That sounds great ... but I'll have to talk to my mother first.'

'While I'm working, you can enjoy yourself and see the sea.'

Bernard was squirming in his chair as though sitting on an anthill. The three good digits on his left hand were drumming on the tabletop while he scratched his nose with his right hand and frowned. He wasn't used to making snap decisions.

'I'll have to talk to my mother ... The thing is, Monsieur Marechall, I don't like to say it, but she thinks you're a poof.'

'Well, why don't we go and see her together? I'm sure we can make her change her mind.'

'When?'

'How about now? Let's not beat about the bush! Why don't you invite me round for lunch? If there's enough for two there'll be enough for three. We can buy her some flowers, or a cake – or both!'

'I think she'd prefer a bottle of something.'

'I'll take care of it. Tell me where she lives and go and let her know I'm coming. Ladies don't like it when you turn up unannounced.'

There was a definite spark between Simon and the tall Negress lamp. She was just his kind of woman: her full lips made no sound and her big white glass eyes shone with total devotion. He heaved himself up from the sofa to put the raffia lampshade straight, and blew on it to clear the dust, which rose up in a little grey cloud and settled again on a nearby surface. He couldn't resist running his hands over the perfect curves, the breasts, belly and hips of this synthetic wooden body. He had known a woman like this once, in Djibouti ... Safia, yes, that was her name. Just as silent and just as radiant. He had been happy with her. He had even thought of staying. In fact, he almost did end up there for good when a riot broke out.

'You all right there, Monsieur Marechall?'

'I'm fine, yes. Take your time.'

'I just have to toss the salad and I'll be right with you. Mother will be ready in five minutes.'

Bernard's voice seemed to come from much further away

than the shop's storeroom, from a distant land Simon had once known and sometimes regretted leaving. He had been to some weird and wonderful places in his time, visiting pagodas and brothels in Asia, sleeping in huts or under the stars in the African desert, but he had never come across anything like Anaïs's shop before. Time itself seemed to have deserted this nowhere land, for fear of being bored to death. He returned to the sofa, perching on the very edge; for if he had the misfortune to sink right into it, he might never make it out of the quicksand of worn velvet cushions.

Bernard had laid the table with mismatched plates and odd knives and forks. The champagne, a cake box from Baudoin and an already wilting bunch of red roses lay side by side. Bernard emerged from the kitchen, his sleeves rolled up and a tea towel over his shoulder, clutching a bowl of salad.

'Here we are, it's ready! Mother's just coming. The thing is, she likes to look good, and she doesn't have people round very often. Mother? ... Mother?'

'Coming!'

It was a strange, double-pitched voice, like the famous Mongolian singers who can hit the low and high notes at the same time. The vision that appeared afterwards was just as remarkable. Anaïs had 'done herself up', decking her shapeless frame in all her showiest finery: moth-eaten silks, faded lace, oil-stained satin, multi-string bead necklaces, clattering metal bangles, globe-sized earrings, Moroccan slippers with worn-out soles, and a frayed turban. Her face was plastered with a thick layer of make-up.

She leant against the doorframe for a moment, her cartoonish kohl-lined eyes judging the distance between herself and Simon and sizing up any obstacles to avoid on the way. Then, like a bull charging the matador, she puffed out through her nose and lunged forward with her hand held out, her face split by a smile reminiscent of a gash made by a machete in a watermelon.

'*Enchantée, cher monsieur, enchantée*! You're most welcome!'

Simon caught her just in time to stop her tripping over a fold in the rug and smoothly kissed her hand. The patchouli oil she had splashed all over herself could not disguise the lingering smell of rum.

'It's unforgivable of my son not to have warned me! So it'll just be a simple meal, I'm afraid.'

'It's my fault for turning up out of the blue.'

'Not at all, not at all! Do please sit down.'

Bernard just managed to slide a chair under his mother's buttocks in time to avert an accident. It must have been a considerable effort for her to get to the table, as she was short of breath and clutching her chest. She fluttered her false eyelashes, one of which was coming unstuck.

'Goodness me, roses! Champagne! And a Baudoin cake! You shouldn't have!'

'Honestly, it's the least I could do, turning up like this.'

'It's a wonderful surprise. Bernard, would you put these flowers in a vase for me please?'

'What vase?'

'Well, I don't know, just a vase, a jug, something!'

Bernard disappeared off to the back of the shop with the flowers, leaving Simon and Anaïs alone at the table.

Though time had not been kind to her, leaving her with sunken eyes, a mouth twisted in bitterness, slack cheeks, skin as dimpled as a peach kernel and straggly hair falling from her turban, Simon could see this woman must once have been beautiful. There were still traces of gold sparkling in the green of her eyes. But her liver-spotted hands, weighed down with jewelled rings as false as her teeth, were incapable of remaining still. They toyed with her knife and fork, folded and unfolded her napkin. Her restless hands gave away her unease at having no place in the world.

'So you're just passing through Vals?'

'That's right. I was on my way down from Paris and was getting bored with the motorway, so I took the back roads and stopped when I got tired. I ended up here by chance, really.'

'Chance, yes, what a thing ... And where are you staying?'

'The Grand Hôtel de Lyon.'

'Oh, very nice. I used to go there sometimes, way back when, for ... a cup of tea in the lounge. Do they still have the snooker table?'

'Yes, it's still there.'

'Still ...'

He was a good-looking man, this Monsieur Marechall. Handsome and smartly turned out, but a little too cool, too sure of himself, too controlled. When he looked at Anaïs it gave her a jolt, like a shard of glass being jabbed into her back.

He didn't seem like a poof though … so what did he want Bernard for?

'Are you a Scorpio?'

'No, Pisces.'

'Then you must be a Scorpio rising?'

'I have no idea. I know nothing at all about star signs.'

'Scorpio rising, without question. Haven't you ever had your birth chart read?'

'No. I'm not really interested in what the future holds.'

'It's not about the future, it's about now.'

'That doesn't mean much to me either. Your Neg—your lamp is beautiful.'

'Isn't it just? I've had it since …' Her voice trailed off. 'It's made of ebony, you know!'

'I'm sure.'

They both turned to contemplate the exotic goddess wearing a flickering sixty-watt bulb on her head. Simon pictured himself back in the arms of Safia, the sunlight filtering through the shutters and streaking across their bodies as they lay entwined on the hemp-woven bed. The clamour of the street, the dust, the shouts of hawkers … Anaïs was reliving the day when her erstwhile lover, Léo – a dealer in stolen goods, rather than antiques – had carried the black goddess to her on his back, in repayment for a debt. He really was handsome, Léo … As for being ebony, the statue was in fact made of a mixture of resin and sand and had been mass-produced in Saint-Étienne. The factory's stamp was printed on the base. But what did that matter now? Even a miserable past largely compensated for a nonexistent present. Their memories were carved from real ebony. They both jumped when Bernard reappeared.

'I couldn't find a vase so I've put the roses in some water in the sink. Right, we're just about ready. Monsieur Marechall, would you mind opening the champagne? I don't know if I can manage it, with my hand.'

Simon did as he was asked, pouring the sparkling wine into the cheap supermarket glasses while Bernard put radishes, butter and salt onto the table. Anaïs pulled a face.

'Is that all you could find for a starter?'

'Radishes are lovely. They're in season. I tried one and they're not too peppery. So, what shall we drink to?'

Simon lifted his glass.

'Let's drink to your future, young man, and to our pasts, my dear.'

Anaïs contrived a sort of smile and downed her drink in one. They talked about everything and nothing, good times and bad, biting into radishes that tasted of springtime. Anaïs was not impressed with the champagne. It made her feel bloated and failed to get her sloshed quickly enough. So, on some pretext or other she took herself off to the kitchen to take a swig of rum. It was only after her third visit to the kitchen that she began to relax.

'So you want to steal my son.'

'Well, borrow his services. I don't think I'm up to driving all the way to Cap d'Agde. But if you'd rather not ...'

'I couldn't care less. So long as he gets paid ...'

'Of course! I'll even pay half up front. It'll be two days at

58

most and he can call home each night.'

'I don't have a phone. Well, I do, but it's been cut off. Anyway, no one calls me. Bernard, give me some mash, will you, and a bit of breast too. I'm hungry today.'

'I'm glad you've got an appetite. Do you want a bit of crispy skin?'

'No, just the white meat. What exactly is it you do?'

'I have a pest-control business. Getting rid of rats, mice, insects, cockroaches and so on.'

'You must be getting plenty of work. The world's overrun with vermin!'

'Yes, business is pretty good.'

'That's what you should have learnt to do, Bernard, instead of getting your fingers chopped off by those damned machines. You know what? Machines need getting rid of too – they deprive us of our bread and butter. In the old days, everything used to be done by hand. Look at this shawl – pure wool, hand-knitted. Now it's all made in China and they crank out acres of the stuff every day! But there's no contest when it comes to quality. Feel this, go on, feel it! It's twenty years old this shawl and it's just like new!'

Simon ran his finger over the rag Anaïs was holding up to him, solemnly nodding his head in agreement.

'That wasn't made by a machine. That was crafted by human hand, an artisan from the Ardèche – or Sweden or Denmark, I can't remember. His workshop was in Antraigues, he was a pal of Jean Ferrat's. He made everything himself, hats, cardigans, mittens. I think he's dead now. Died of cold, or so I heard ...

Bernard, open a bottle of red to wash down the champagne.'

'Don't you think you've—'

'No, I don't. Off you go and find a bottle, like I said.'

Anaïs was melting like a candle, her elbows sliding towards the edge of the table. Her bloodshot eyes stared dead ahead, like brake lights jammed on in the face of a hazard, a hole in the road or a gaping abyss.

'Are you sure you're not a queer?'

'Quite sure. I just need a driver. I met your son and I trust him, that's all there is to it.'

'Uh-huh ... It's just that I'm his mother, I know him. He's so ... It's like he was born yesterday.'

'That's what makes him so likeable.'

'And means he's always being taken for a ride. Couldn't you take him on in your company? He's missing a couple of fingers but he's not lazy.'

'The thing is, I'm about to sell my business and retire.'

'Ah, what a shame. You think you're in luck and then ...'

'I'm sorry, I ...'

Anaïs slumped forward with a snore, her forehead landing in her plate and her arms lolling either side of the chair. Bernard came back in holding the cake on a plate and a bottle tucked under his arm.

'This is Lou Pisadou cake, a speciality of Vals ... Mother! Christ, what's the matter with her?'

'She's asleep.'

'She's drunk too much. She's not used to it and whenever she has someone over, she drinks gallons so obviously ... I'm so sorry, Monsieur Marechall.'

'Don't worry. We should probably put her to bed. I'll help you.'

'OK, thank you.'

They laid her on her bed in a cubbyhole that seemed to Simon like a sort of crypt. After tucking her in, they went back to the table.

'Can I still cut you a slice of cake?'

'No, thank you, I'm full. It was a very good lunch.'

'A coffee then?'

'No, I think I'll head back to my hotel for a nap.'

'It's not her fault, you know. She never has company.'

'There's no need to apologise, Bernard. Your mother is a lovely lady, perhaps just a little over-emotional. We got along very well. Now, here's half your pay. So I'll see you tomorrow at nine o'clock, at my hotel?'

'Nine o'clock without fail, Monsieur Marechall!'

They shook hands and Simon exchanged one last glance with the Negress lamp before leaving.

'Now that's what I call a motor! There's a proper engine under that bonnet! And German too, they don't come more reliable.'

Bernard was as ecstatic as a little boy who had just been given his first pedal car. He drove well, smoothly negotiating every corner – and God knows there were enough of them on this road. The rolling hills were tinged mauve and pink in the morning light. The car was so quiet, the suspension so perfect, it felt as though they were sitting still while the countryside sped past.

Although he had taken his pills, Simon had not slept a wink all night. The pains which had abated for a while had suddenly started again. Bernard really was a godsend. Were it not for him, Simon would never have been able to get on the road today. And Bernard's youthful enthusiasm cheered him up. He was already feeling a little better. The clouds glowed with the pastel blue and pink shades of sugared almonds. Something odd had happened yesterday as he walked back to his hotel after that unusual lunch with Bernard's mother. Rue Jean-Jaurès was deserted at that time of day. As he passed the church, he heard a mobile phone ringing from inside; for some reason, the doors were wide open. The phone rang and rang, but no one picked it up. His curiosity piqued, Simon went inside. The church was empty. The phone was vibrating on a prayer stool. He picked it up and raised it to his ear. Three times he said, 'Hello?'

His voice bounced off the ceiling vaults like a trapped bird, but there was no reply. He put the phone back where he had found it. The church seemed huge to him, though it was actually quite modest in size. Three rays of light – red, blue and yellow – shone through the ugly stained-glass windows, converging in a multicoloured pool at his feet. He had the strongest feeling that something had passed him by, that he had missed some important appointment. It was ridiculous but he could have sworn the phone call was meant for him. He felt abandoned and alone, surrounded by nothingness. He almost ran out of the church. Maybe that was what had kept him awake all night.

'If we keep on at this rate, we'll be there in less than two hours. Are you OK, Monsieur Marechall?'

'I'm fine, I'm fine. Where are we now?'

'Le Teil.'

'Let's stop for a minute. I need to use the toilet.'

They pulled up in front of the train station and dived into the first bar they came to.

'What would you like, Monsieur Marechall?'

'Anything, a coffee.'

63

Bernard watched him disappear off to the toilets. He looked pale, his brow dripping with sweat. It was a pity; Bernard was in holiday mood. Twirling the keys of the Mercedes for all to see, he casually asked for two coffees and two croissants. The waitress winked at him and smiled. The joys of having money ... He stretched his legs out under the table, clasped his hands behind his head and stared up at the ceiling with its fake beams. There was only one other customer, a tall, skinny, spidery man perched on a bar stool, his gaze lost in the celestial void that filled the window. In his right hand he held a half-pint, in his left a cigarette. Spinning out the hours. He didn't bat an eyelid when a petite blonde woman carrying a baby in an orange blanket stormed in and started screaming at him.

'You fucking bastard!'

The spidery man let his left arm be shaken, but clung fast to the half-pint in his other hand.

'Give me the keys, you bastard!'

'The keys are gone.'

'What do you mean, "gone"?'

'The bailiffs came this morning. There's no flat, no keys, no nothing.'

He put an end to the discussion by downing the rest of his beer. The young woman opened and closed her mouth over and over again, without making a sound.

'But ... You told me you'd paid the rent, you said it was all sorted.'

'Well, it wasn't. So shut your mouth and piss off.'

The owner looked up from his newspaper and frowned.

The woman swivelled round, clocked Bernard, plonked the child on his lap, grabbed an ashtray and lunged at the man. It was 9.30 a.m. on a sunny day in Le Teil. The owner grudgingly came out from behind the counter armed with a cosh. His weary expression showed he had seen all this many times before.

'Right, out of here now. Sort out your domestics somewhere else! Go on! Out!'

'I haven't paid for my half!'

'It's on the house. Now fuck off before I call the police.'

A warm liquid ran onto Bernard's lap. The kid was emptying itself like a leaky hot water bottle.

Simon pulled the chain and the toilet bowl was spotless again, all traces of the blood he had vomited wiped clean. The light coming through the window coursed through his body like fresh milk. He felt empty and hollow, but better. Sometimes the illness loosened its grip on him, like an executioner tired of delivering blows. It would be back for more, no mistake, but not right away. They were getting to know each other rather well, him and his illness.

Coming out of the toilets, he was astonished to find Bernard in Madonna pose, cradling a baby.

'What's all this?'

'I don't know! A couple are having a row. It's peed on me and I haven't got a change of trousers.'

The infant, swaddled in its orange blanket, looked as bewildered as Bernard.

'What on earth's going on?'

The woman was now grappling with the nineteen-stone bulk of the bar owner, who was blocking her way.

'Just let me past, dickhead! My kid, I just need to get my kid and I'll never come back to this shithole again!'

She managed to squeeze past him, cross the room and retrieve the child without a word of thanks to Bernard, then stomped out with a determined stride. The coffee had gone cold. Simon gulped his down in one go. Bernard's arms were still held in a cradling position.

'For a moment you made me think of St Christopher carrying Jesus across the river. It bodes well, since he's the patron saint of drivers.'

'I stink!'

'Come on, let's sort you out.'

Simon paid the bill.

'Sorry about that,' said the owner. 'There's more and more of that sort round here. Scroungers, living off benefits we slog to pay for. And then they go and breed, God only knows why.'

Bernard walked with his legs slightly apart. Simon steered him into a passably stylish shop – quite possibly the only one in town.

'We need a suit for this young man. Something smart but not too "old".'

Bernard stared at Simon in amazement.

'A suit?'

'Well, you'll need one sooner or later. Anyway it's for my

benefit, not yours. We can't have you driving a Mercedes dressed like that. People will think you've stolen it.'

The jacket was a perfect fit, but it felt to Bernard as rigid as a suit of armour. He squirmed his way into the driving seat, trying not to crumple it.

'I've never worn any of this formal stuff before, you know?'

'It'll be fine, just try not to think about it. Now tell me, what are you going to do when we get to the sea?'

'Well ... sit down and look at it, I suppose.'

'Good idea. I envy you, seeing the sea for the first time.'

The plane trees lining the road broke up the light. The air coming in through the windows smelt of distant shores. Bernard drove one-handed, his head cocked slightly to the left.

'Monsieur Marechall, can I ask you something?'

'Yes, what is it?'

'Were you unwell earlier?'

'I was just a little light-headed. Remembering Africa, times gone by ... old age ... Hang on, what do you think you're doing? Why are we stopping?'

Bernard had pulled up on the verge and twisted in his seat.

'Back there, behind the red car! It's the girl from the café with her baby. The tall guy's hitting her!'

'So?'

'So we should do something.'

'Don't get involved. It's none of your business. Now drive.'

'I can't, Monsieur Marechall. The kid peed on me, it's like we're family.'

'Family? For God's sake! No, you stay there behind the wheel and keep the engine running. I'll go, it'll be quicker.'

He was right, it did not take long. Everything was played out in the rear-view mirror: Monsieur Marechall walking calmly towards the red car, hands in the pockets of his raincoat. Reaching the scene of the argument, he says a couple of words to the girl who begins running towards the Mercedes, hugging her child to her chest. The tall guy lifts his arm and Monsieur Marechall takes something out of his pocket. The tall guy lifts his other arm and disappears into the ditch as if by magic. The girl with the baby scrambles into the car, her face beetroot red, hair dishevelled, panting, wild-eyed; Monsieur Marechall walks back just as calmly, gets into the car and does up his seat belt with a sigh.

'Well, what are you waiting for? Go!' He turned to the woman in the back. 'Where shall we drop you, Madame?'

'I ... I don't know, down the road.'

Shortly after Montélimar they had to stop at a service station, the little girl's ear-splitting cries signalling she was hungry. While the young mother took her baby off to the toilets, Simon leant against the car door, smoking a cigarette, and Bernard kicked around a battered Orangina can. Simon stubbed his cigarette out under his foot and turned up his collar.

'Let's drop them at Nîmes.'

'Why Nîmes?'

'Because we're not going to have them trail along with us all the way to China. And Nîmes is very nice.'

'But what if they don't know anybody in Nîmes?'

'It's not my problem. We helped them out – what more do you want? I've got work to do and we've already wasted a lot of time.'

'You're right, Monsieur Marechall. Got to get to work.'

Bernard adroitly struck the can on the volley, sending it into a bush. He threw his arms up.

'Goal! ... Monsieur Marechall?'

'Yes?'

'How did you handle that guy?'

'Which guy?'

'The one who was hitting her. He looked a lot stronger than you.'

'I don't know. He must have seen I had no time to mess around. Right, what the hell's taking them so long?'

'He didn't get back out of the ditch ...'

'He must have landed awkwardly. Ah, here they are! Let's go.'

Babies are like open-ended tubes, filled up at the top and emptied at the bottom. Since this baby had just been filled up at the service station, it emptied itself around Avignon. Even with the windows open, the smell was overpowering. Simon knew the stench of shit, blood and rot all too well; it was the smell of war, and he was used to it. But something about this poo, mingled with wafts of sour milk, was getting to him. It was not a horrible smell, exactly; it was a farmyard odour, the whiff of the compost heap, a primeval human memory that aroused a certain nostalgia. But these two impromptu passengers were really beginning to try his patience. They had not been planned for and Simon hated surprises.

'Will you stop shaking her around? It's making her give off even more gas.'

'I'm not shaking her, I'm rocking her. She'll cry if I don't.'

'That's all we need.'

Bernard had said nothing but could feel the tension rising.

'What's the baby's name?' he asked.

'Violette.'

'Oh, that's a pretty name!'

Simon shrugged his shoulders and ground his teeth.

'Doesn't smell like violets, that's for sure!'

'Well, she's a baby, Monsieur Marechall, it's only natural.'

'Only natural? What about death cap mushrooms, they're natural too, and hemlock, and a lot of other poisons besides! The world's full of natural children. Three-quarters of them should never have seen the light of day.'

'How can you say that?'

'Because it's true. Half the planet's dying of hunger. The poor should just eat their offspring. I mean, it's protein, isn't it? That's the way to cure starvation.'

'That's a bit much, Monsieur Marechall. People eating their own children!'

'Well, why not?'

Wriggling about in her dirty nappy, Violette began to screech. Her mother, Fiona, held her more tightly.

'That's a horrible thing to say. She heard everything ... Don't worry, poppet, Mummy will never eat you ... She needs changing but I've run out of nappies.'

Simon clapped his hand to his forehead and took deep breaths to calm his nerves.

'Here's what we're going to do. In a quarter of an hour we'll be in Avignon. We're going to drop you off at a chemist's, or a supermarket, wherever, and we're going to say goodbye. We all go our separate ways. Understood?'

71

'I don't know anybody in Avignon ... What am I going to do with the baby?'

'Do what you like! You're young, you're not bad-looking, you'll find another man like the last one and so it'll go on. Bernard, stop as soon as you can; we've already wasted too much time.'

'Right, Monsieur Marechall.'

On the back seat, the child had fallen asleep, her body floppy and mouth wide open. Fiona was snivelling quietly, tears glistening on her cheeks. Bernard kept glancing back at her in the rear-view mirror. It hurt him to see her like that. She reminded him of that girl ... Liliane, who had only stayed at the factory a few days. Long enough for him to fall in love with her. Nothing had really happened between them other than sharing a lunchbox once and grabbing a coffee at the bar of Le Penalty. Even so, it had been a love affair. Fiona had that same vacant look in her eyes, the same sickly skin that bruised easily, the aloofness of those who are just passing through.

Ma môme, ell' joue pas les starlettes / Ell' met pas des lunettes / De soleil / Ell' pos' pas pour les magazines / Ell' travaille en usine / A Créteil.

My girl don't put on airs and graces / She don't wear sunglasses / In the shade / She don't pose for no magazines / She works in a factory / in Créteil.

Good old Jean Ferrat. He knew how to talk about that stuff.

'Bernard, we just went right past a chemist's. Why didn't you stop?'

'I didn't see it until too late. There's a lorry on my tail.'

They could have been anywhere. The outskirts of towns look the same in every part of the world. Uncertain places, business parks and shopping centres, *terra incognita*, no man's lands cluttered with neon signs promising eternal happiness to whoever buys this or that product. You know you're alive when you're buying stuff. Judging from the rows of parked cars lined up with military precision, heaven could wait. Here, it was possible to live and die just like in real life, in a fraction of the time.

'Park up, Bernard. They have everything here. Well, goodbye, Fiona. Good luck.'

Fiona's gaze seemed to fall elsewhere, a place where nobody ever looked. Her hair was piled messily on top of her head. She played with a loose strand, twisting it around her finger.

'I haven't got any money.'

Simon puffed out loudly through his nostrils like a buffalo, scrunching up his eyes.

'Bernard, here's fifty euros. Give it to her and take them to die somewhere else, OK?'

'OK, Monsieur Marechall. I'll walk them to the entrance.'

'Fine.'

Through the windscreen, he watched them walking towards Auchan. They looked like a happy little family pushing their trolley along. The sun was shining into his lap. He leant back against the headrest and rubbed his temples.

'One day I came into the world ... and then what?'

He felt a sudden sense of emptiness coupled with an

awareness of the sheer incongruity of the situation. What the hell was he doing sitting in the middle of nowhere, waiting for some gangling halfwit to come back? He had a contract to carry out and he had never to this day failed to do the job. He was feeling much better; he did not need anybody else. Those three were all of the same ilk. They would get by just fine without him.

Simon slid behind the wheel and started the engine. Where the hell was the exit? There were arrows pointing in every direction, but they never seemed to lead anywhere. Driving round in circles, he inevitably, fatally, ended up back at square one. Bernard was standing with Fiona and Violette, holding a huge pack of nappies under his arm and watching unfazed and entirely unquestioningly as Simon pulled up alongside them.

'I was going to fill up but there's a queue. You get back behind the wheel, Bernard. Get in then.'

The motorway carved its way through a moonscape of scrubland and dry rock. It was eleven o'clock and the sun was beating down relentlessly.

'... and while you're working, I'll find them a place to stay, somewhere nice but not too expensive. What do you think, Monsieur Marechall?'

'I don't give a damn, I just want them out of my hair.'

'Don't worry, Monsieur Marechall. I'll pay for it out of my wages.'

In the back, Fiona was shaking her head as the arid hillsides flashed past.

'Can we put some music on? It'll help send Violette to sleep.'

'Do you mind, Monsieur Marechall?'

On Radio Nostalgie, Dalida was belting out her tear-jerking classic, 'Ciao Amore' ... Simon was asleep before the baby.

'Time to wake up, Monsieur Marechall. We're nearly there.'

Simon opened one eye and closed it again almost immediately, assailed by the sunlight daubing the windscreen with a lurid carousel of colours. Past a certain age, sleep becomes a rare luxury, given up reluctantly. His mind had been empty of dreams or nightmares, which seemed to him like the most perfect state of grace, as though he had never existed at all. But now he was forced to re-inhabit his pitiful skin that sagged over tired muscles and stuck to creaking bones; to regain his basic thoughts and functions, which at that moment meant nothing to him.

'Where to now?'

'Le Grau d'Agde. Go right, along the River Hérault.'

'Oh yes, it's signposted ... Ah, look. Isn't that sweet?'

'What?'

'The two of them sleeping in the back. It's like a First Communion picture.'

'Do you remember what I said? I don't want to see them again. You're going to find us a decent place to stay. We're moving on tomorrow.'

'Don't worry, Monsieur Marechall. No probs. Here we are, this is Le Grau whatsitsname.'

'Right then, drop me off here. We'll meet at ... four o'clock sharp, at the aquarium, OK?'

'I'll be there, without fail. Oh, Monsieur Marechall, I meant to say ... I'm just so happy to be here, thank you.'

'The sea's straight on, at the end of the road. Four o'clock.'

The car drove off, leaving Simon standing slightly disorientated on the pavement, pounded by the force of the sun. For a fraction of a second he wished he could change places with the big schmuck who thought he was on holiday, even if it meant having two fingers missing. He only stepped back into his shady world once he had put his dark glasses on.

He bought thirteen red roses at the first florist's he came to.

'Thirteen? People usually buy a dozen.'

'Not me.'

While the florist – a pretty enough girl, despite her repaired harelip – made up the bouquet, the shop's warm, humid atmosphere and exotic fragrances transported Simon back to the Indonesian forests he had so loved. He could have stayed there for ever, too ... He could have lived anywhere but here, in fact. Funny how things turned out.

'That'll be twenty-six euros, please.'

Outside the shop, he looked at his map. Impasse du Lavandin

was only a few streets away. He did not pass a single person on his way. The theme tune of a German soap opera floated from open windows, a daily dose to numb the tired brains of the local retirees. They lived in big houses and apartment blocks with fragrant-sounding names like Les Acacias, Les Mimosas and Les Pins. In reality it smelt more like a cemetery, with hints of barbecue smoke and sulphur ointment used for hernia bandages.

Number 4, Impasse du Lavandin was a detached house built in no discernible style, a sort of 1960s shoebox with a disproportionately large neo-classical terrace tacked on to it. It was surrounded by a high wall topped with shards of coloured glass set into the concrete. Beside the gate, above a letterbox marked 'J.-P. Bornay', an intercom invited callers to buzz and give their name or else beware of the dog. Said dog was depicted on a ceramic tile, tongue lolling, eager fangs bared. Simon pressed the red button. A crackly voice answered, drowned out by wild yapping.

'Who is it?'

'Monsieur Marechall. I'm a colleague of your husband Jean-Pierre's. He asked me to give you something.'

'What is it?'

'Flowers, I think.'

'Flowers? Are you joking?'

'If you wouldn't mind letting me in, I'll just drop them off. I'm in a bit of a hurry.'

She, on the other hand, seemed in no hurry at all, making Simon wait a good five minutes before the gate was buzzed open.

Asymmetrical flagstones formed a hopscotch path across the freshly mown lawn, dotted with clumps of spiky succulents and a random assortment of newly planted flowers. Behind a metal grille, the frosted, probably bulletproof door was ajar, letting out the jabbering of a television along with a hyperactive Yorkshire terrier. The flaccid face of a woman appeared in the shadow of the doorway, the bags under her eyes betraying her worries. Simon proffered his bouquet with a smile. She did not take it straight away, eyeing him with suspicion, her nostrils twitching.

'Isn't there a card with them?'

'Oh, yes, there is! I'm so sorry, it's in my pocket. Do you mind?'

She gingerly took the flowers, while Simon took out of his pocket Jean-Pierre Bornay's last message to his wife: a bullet between the eyes. She toppled backwards into the dark hallway, her body strewn with thirteen red roses. The dog chased around in circles a few times, trying to understand the rules of this strange game, then stopped to cover his mistress's face in long tongue strokes. Simon knelt down, snapped a rose from its stem, slipped it into his buttonhole – a little tradition of his – and stood back up, wincing. With the butt of his gun he knocked out the dog, which had started to claw at his trouser leg. So there it was, Jean-Pierre Bornay was free to be joined in holy matrimony with his secretary. Another job well done. Simon could bow out honourably.

The further he got from this geriatric neighbourhood, whose residents generally died of their own accord, the livelier the streets became. Car horns beeped and people hurried by, jostling, cursing or paying no attention to each other. All was right with the world.

Simon could not find a single telephone box in working order, now they had been superseded by mobile phones. He went into a café to call the man who had hired him.

'It's done. Meet me at five o'clock at the aquarium ... What do you mean, you can't? ... I'm not happy about this ... As soon as it opens tomorrow, nine thirty, and no messing about!'

Though considerably annoyed by this setback, Simon never-theless sat down at a table and ordered a glass of Suze. This, along with the thirteen red roses, was an essential element of an unbending ritual. He got it from his father, a miner from Doullens, who had taught him always to do his best and shown him the satisfaction of a job well done. It was a kind of tribute to this worthy man, snatched from him when he was just twelve, his lungs destroyed by silicosis. If his father had not expressly forbidden him from following in his footsteps, down into the bowels of the earth, Simon might have been a mining engineer now, or dead, or on the dole. As a child, Simon had lapped up the mysterious tales of subterranean life his father told him, coughing up coal dust into his handkerchief. The firedamp explosions, the sense of brotherhood, the strikes – it was like something out of Zola or Jules Verne. It must have been a wish to experience something similar that had prompted Simon to join the army at the age of eighteen. Everyone had been disappointed because he was a star pupil, destined for great things. But what kind of adult would he be if he did not fulfil his childhood dreams?

Though he moved quickly up the ranks, he soon realised that opportunities for real adventure were few and far between. Although he had the chance to do some digging, it was not to find buried treasure but to bury rigid corpses, bundled up by the dozen like human firewood. It was no more glamorous than working at an undertaker's.

The Suze seemed more bitter than usual, the noises around him more acute, the colours more vivid. Everything was too strong for him, including the relentless waves of hot and cold sweeping over him. It was coming on again. Staring into the pure white porcelain urinal calmed him briefly, as he stood emptying his bladder next to a man in a blue tracksuit.

'Lieutenant?'

'I'm sorry?'

'Aren't you Lieutenant Marechall?'

'No, I'm afraid you're mistaken.'

'I'm sorry. I thought for a moment ...'

'It's fine, these things happen. Goodbye.'

Picot. He had just pissed next to that arsehole Picot, a play-it-safe mercenary and small-time killer Simon had nevertheless pulled out of a swamp in Burma. There was no denying it: the world was closing in on Simon and soon even he would be surplus to it.

The shark was drowning its sorrows inside its glass cage. It turned this way and that for no apparent reason, taking no notice of the opaline jellyfish and shoals of multicoloured fish swimming out from clumps of soft seaweed. There was not much to choose between aquatic life and life on earth; either could be equally boring. The proof was in the amphibians which had dithered between the two for thousands of years without ever making their minds up, or the Valium-drugged crocodiles whose sleepy eyes peeked above the surface of muddy pools. Like Simon, who stood watching them, all these creatures seemed to be on standby, waiting for something that was always just out of reach. Over-excited kids pressed their noses against the glass, banging their horrid chubby little hands against the walls of the tanks. Their shrieks ruined the silence of this other world. From the looks on the faces of their harassed parents, it was clear many would gladly throw their offspring to the piranhas. The world might well end in the same murky green waters that spawned humanity.

'Are you OK, Monsieur Marechall? You don't look too good.'

'It's the lighting in here; it makes everyone look washed out. Have you found a hotel?'

'Even better! Shall we go now?'

The shock of stepping from the gloom into bright daylight made Simon burn up. He staggered back to the car.

'You'll see, Monsieur Marechall, it's a dream spot!'

'I have no interest in dreaming, I just want to go to sleep. I'm tired.'

'No probs! You'll be in paradise in no time.'

They drove for no more than quarter of an hour. Simon had closed his eyes, opening them again only when he felt the car slowing down.

'What the hell is this? A campsite?'

'Not just any campsite, Monsieur Marechall, a three-star campsite. And don't worry, we're not going to be sleeping under canvas.'

Beneath towering pine trees lined up like soldiers, they passed an array of caravans, from the tiniest to the most palatial, before pulling up outside a mobile home as warm and inviting as a fridge.

'Is this supposed to be a joke?'

'Just wait until you see it all, Monsieur Marechall. The sea's just behind us, fifty yards away. It's got all mod cons and it's way cheaper than a hotel.'

'I don't give a damn how much it costs! I asked you to book a hotel!'

'Don't get cross, Monsieur Marechall. If you don't like it,

we can go. But just come and have a look. It's better than a hotel – it's got a kitchen and a shower, just like home.'

Simon did not have the strength to put up a fight. Tangled up in the threads that were just about holding him together, he trailed behind Bernard.

'So here's the kitchen. It's got a hotplate, microwave, fridge, hot and cold running water. Bathroom, with towels and everything. That's your room there. Just pull the screen across and you've got it all to yourself. I'll sleep in the hall, there's a fold-out sofa bed. Isn't it great? Have a look out the window – you can see the beach and the sea ... You were right – it's really something, all that water, it's amazing!'

Simon sank onto the bed, his arms outstretched. Resistance was futile.

'You're not very well, are you, Monsieur Marechall? I'll leave you to rest. I'll sort everything out. I went to check out the shops – what do you think about having mussels for supper? ... Take your time. I'm just going down to the beach to see Fiona and the baby and then I'll get some food in.'

'They're here too?'

'Not in the same caravan – I'm not stupid! I've rented one for them just next door. Now you lie back and relax, you'll be snug as a bug in a jug.'

'In a rug.'

'Yes, if you like. Happy?'

'Delirious. Now bugger off.'

'OK, rest up, Monsieur Marechall, see you later. You know, I just can't thank you enough for all this, the sea, this whole adventure ...'

'Get out.'

The bed was hard and, even with the bottle-green chenille blanket over him, Simon was cold. The pillow was as comfortable as cardboard. None of it mattered now; Simon's sole desire was to escape from his body, which he managed to do after swallowing a handful of pills that shut off his brain with a watertight seal. Really it was no worse being here than anywhere else. He did not feel bad or good; he felt nothing at all. The lingering stench of cleaning products, used to scrub away all traces of the previous occupants, left Simon with a curious feeling of virginity.

Simon did not really sleep. It was a kind of semi-slumber, bobbing just beneath the surface, which left him wishing he could grow scales and inhabit the aquarium. The light of the setting sun made the room blush girlishly. His watch gave the time as 6.12 p.m., and he accepted it.

Outside, the breeze carried the tang of pine and salt water. When Simon reached the beach he did as everyone does; he took off his shoes and socks, rolled up his trousers and made for the water.

There it was, waiting faithfully. The sea glimmered with copper shards of sun, dribbling white foam and babbling the time away with idle chatter. Standing upright in a world without vertical lines, Simon dropped down on the sand and laid his shoes out next to him as though waiting for Father Christmas to fill them. A red ball bounced close by. A little boy and his father came running after it. They looked happy – the ball especially. With a burst of imagination, the sun had turned a hopelessly clear sky into an engaging spectacle, taking the lonely little cloud no storm had wanted and trimming it with gold.

'All right?'

Fiona loomed behind him in silhouette like a harbinger of doom, hunchbacked under her daughter's grip.

'What do you care? Where's Bernard?'

'Gone shopping. Can I sit down?'

'It's a beach, it's public property.'

She was wearing a red T-shirt and white shorts. She had nice legs. The little girl was staring at the horizon as solemnly as a child can contemplate such things. The sky and sea were coming together like the two edges of a bloody wound.

'Bernard's nice, isn't he?'

Simon made no comment.

'Are you related?'

'No.'

'Oh, I thought you were. It must be because he looks up to you. He walks the way you do, has the same frown ... You end up look-ing like the people you're fond of, don't you think?'

Simon was studying his feet, which were so pale they were practically blue, with a bunion on the left big toe and calloused nails. His ankles were ringed with the imprint of his sock elastic. He buried them in the still-warm sand. If he had been alone, he might have interred himself up to the neck.

'Why don't you like me?'

'Why should I? I have no interest in you.'

'Why did you get me out of that fix then?'

'Because of Bernard. He would have made a pig's ear of it. I didn't have time to waste. Now, would you mind leaving me the hell alone?'

'Fine! You were right to hide your feet, they're disgusting.'

Fiona's buttocks left two perfectly round craters in the grey sand beside him.

On the dot of eight o'clock, the TV news signature tune spread like a powder trail down the row of caravans, the newsreader's chubby face replicated endlessly. It was a mild evening and most of the holidaymakers were eating outdoors. Bernard was at the stove, Fiona was laying the table and Simon was trying to outstare Violette, who was propped up with cushions on a camping chair. All around them, corks were popping, ripples of laughter broke out and cooking smells mingled in the evening air. The whole situation was so bizarre that Simon had not even tried to protest when Bernard told him there would be three and a half of them for dinner. There was nothing to be said, nothing to be done except sulk. He felt like a serious stage actor who had wandered onto the set of a slushy movie. He could not follow the plot, but it was too late to back out now. The mischievous director had already called, 'Action!'

Bernard brought over the mussels and doled out generous portions. He and Fiona were like an old married couple, sharing habits, exchanging knowing winks and making thoughtful gestures, with Fiona helping him as he struggled to open the mussels with his bandaged hand. Simon swallowed three or four and drank half the bottle of white wine by himself. His forehead creased in a frown, he sat wondering what casting error had landed him here, a stranger in paradise. By odd coincidence, it had just been announced on the news that Gloria Lasso had died. Her biggest hit was none other than 'Étrangère au Paradis', the soundtrack to the four years he had spent in the Aurès mountains of Algeria, hunting down *fellagha* militants. The song had been on wherever he went – in the barracks, in tents and in brothels, trickling from the transistor radios glued to every soldier's ear, their stomachs heavy with nostalgia and warm beer.

'Who was Gloria Lasso?' asked Fiona.

'Dunno. More mussels?'

It all seemed so distant that Simon began to wonder if it had really happened. Most likely it had, since that was where he had learnt to kill. Everything was going so fast, even the present day had to be glimpsed through a rear-view mirror.

'Aren't you going to finish your mussels, Monsieur Marechall?'

'I'm too tired. I'm going to bed. Don't forget, eight o'clock tomorrow morning!'

'Without fail, Monsieur Marechall. Good night.'

He had barely made it into the caravan when Bernard and Fiona heard him coughing and throwing up in the bathroom.

'Do you think it was my mussels?'

'No, they're lovely. It's him – he's not well, your Monsieur Marechall.'

'What's wrong with him?'

'Death, that's his disease. You can see it on his face and it's nothing new. That man has never had feelings for anyone.'

'I think you're wrong there. I think he likes me a lot.'

'Maybe ... Maybe he loved someone once but she turned him down and he never got over it. Watch out. A drowning man never wants to go down alone.'

The sea and the sky, vying with each other in their vastness, traded handfuls of stars.

'I'm a bit chilly. Violette's asleep; I think I'll head indoors.'

'I'll walk you back.'

A few TVs still hummed, but most had been turned off. With the little girl in his arms, Bernard felt he could go anywhere, do anything. He took strength from the warm, squidgy human ball of dough he held against him – and the sight of Fiona's moonlike buttocks strutting in her tight white shorts.

'You can come in if you want.'

'That would be nice, but I can't. It's not that I don't want to, it's just I'm a bit worried about Monsieur Marechall. He might need me. See you tomorrow then?'

'See you tomorrow.'

Fiona's lips ...

Monsieur Marechall was sprawled across the dishevelled bed wearing only his boxers, open-mouthed and scrawny as a giant skinned rabbit. Just as he was used to doing for his mother,

Bernard put him straight, slid a pillow under his head and pulled the blanket up to his chin. Bernard wasn't sleepy. If life was as kind to him every day as it had been today, he would never sleep again. Excitement bubbled through his veins like champagne. It was even better than the day he'd passed his driving test, because this time the only thing he was drunk on was pure, unalloyed happiness.

Once he had made sure everything was in order, Bernard went back down to the beach. The sand was crisscrossed with the footprints of thousands of children, adults and dogs, which seemed almost to come alive in the moonlight. It was as moving a sight as the red clay handprints discovered on the walls of prehistoric caves. Not as ancient, of course, but renewed and immortalised with each passing day. A white plastic bag was lifted high on a gust of wind like a miniature hot air balloon, and then disappeared behind a bush. This thing with Fiona could turn into something, a relationship. And what was more, she already had a baby he had not even needed to have a hand in making. Things with Monsieur Marechall were not so rosy, though. He was worried about him. What was this 'death' disease Fiona had talked about? Something he had picked up through his job? The truth was, he was really quite attached to the old grouch. Without a father of his own, he had to find a substitute, and Monsieur Marechall fitted the bill.

Bernard lay down on the sand, which moulded snugly around his body. The waves were lapping, the stars whispering. Everything was as it should be, perfectly still, until he caught sight of a stupid green satellite flashing in the distance, reminding him that time was passing. Monsieur Marechall had an important meeting in the morning, at nine thirty on the dot, and then ... then it would be time to say goodbye to Fiona and Violette and he would be back to square one, in Vals-les-Bains. He didn't fancy the prospect of going back to his humdrum existence one bit. Except ... he could drive Monsieur Marechall back to Vals and maybe, if he had done a good job, he might even get a bonus, in which case there was nothing to stop him coming back here. Fiona's caravan was booked for three weeks. If he set his mind to it, he could make a lot of headway in three weeks ...

The moon grinned down on him as he built up his little Lego bricks of hope.

'And have you ever been to the bottom of the sea, Monsieur Marechall?'

'I went diving in the Red Sea once.'

'Ooh ... is it really red?'

'No.'

'What's it like then?'

'Just like where we're going now.'

'The aquarium, OK ... The reason I asked is because I had this dream last night that I was down there, at the bottom of the sea. I could breathe just like normal. Everything was slow, quiet and warm, like being inside someone's tummy. There were other creatures down there and weird wavy seaweed. We all swam around, brushing past each other and saying hello. It was so calm, so – I dunno – peaceful. Then suddenly I was being pulled to the surface. I was flapping around but there was nothing I could do to stop it. My mouth was full of bubbles when WHAM! I hit the surface of the water which must have been frozen or something; it was smooth and hard like a mirror. I was banging my hands against it but it was no use – there was no way up or down.'

'So then what?'

'Nothing. I woke up.'

'Dreams are so stupid.'

'You're right, Monsieur Marechall, they are. Why do we have them?'

'Because real life isn't enough. Park over there, just in front, and leave the engine running. If I'm not back in ten minutes, come down and find me.'

'The same place as yesterday, in front of the shark?'

'The same place.'

'Are you sure you don't want me to come with you? You don't look very well.'

'Ten minutes, OK?'

Only the thickness of the windscreen stood between dream and reality. It might have been a hangover from Bernard's dream, but people, objects and animals seemed to be moving in slow motion before him. No sooner had the guard opened the gate to the aquarium than Monsieur Marechall disappeared inside.

There is nothing as boring as someone telling you their dreams. Simon screwed the silencer onto the barrel of his gun and waited, concealed in a dark corner. The shark continued its endless circling, indifferent to everything including its own existence. The minutes dripped by, like water from clothes on a washing line. On laundry days, Simon used to sit and watch his mother hanging out the washing in the yard. Her apron pocket was filled with wooden pegs; she always kept one between her teeth. Shirts, overalls, long johns and faded woollens flapped like the flags of a ship in distress – or rather a rudimentary raft. There was not a single item that had not been darned or patched. He was ashamed to see their pitiful, intimate garments aired in public. Yet the same show was being staged in every back garden along the terrace of small brick houses. Scrub as they might, the hard-working housewives could never get their laundry clean under that soot-filled sky.

A figure appeared at the top of the stairs. It was not Jean-Pierre Bornay. He was too tall and thin. Simon gripped his gun and took a step forward. The man noticed him and stopped in his tracks, like a heron that has spotted a fish.

'Marechall?'

'Where's Bornay?'

'Couldn't make it. Sent me instead.'

Simon allowed the stand-in to come within a metre of him. Looking at him straight on was like seeing a face in profile; only one eye was visible, as round and cold as that of the shark.

'Have you got the envelope?'

'Yes, here.'

He held it out to Simon with his left hand, but his right remained out of sight.

'Open it.'

The stranger's eye grew even rounder and his mouth

twitched nervously. Simon deflected the gun pointing at him and simultaneously fired through his pocket. The stray bullet struck the piranha tank, which shattered like a star and finally burst, spewing out an almost solid wave of seaweed, roots, shards of glass and flailing fish. The man clutched his stomach and fell first to his knees, then onto his side. Simon leant down to pick up the sodden envelope. As he straightened up, he saw Bernard on the third step, rooted to the spot with horror at the scene before him. There was a man squirming at Monsieur Marechall's feet, soaked in red water and surrounded by funny little fish, all jagged-toothed mouths and tails flapping around in the darkness. An alarm began ringing. Monsieur Marechall grabbed Bernard by the elbow and pulled him away.

'Move, now!'

As they barged up the stairs, they passed the dazed guard who stammered, 'What's going on? What's happened?'

The shock of stepping from the gloom into bright daylight made them both teeter. They groped their way back to the car like blind men and clambered inside.

'Drive, damn it! Go!'

Bernard stalled twice before the car joined the flow of traffic.

'Where to, Monsieur Marechall? Where to now?'

'To the campsite. Go back to the campsite.'

Simon was breathing heavily through his nose and speaking through his teeth, his jaws clamped shut.

The town had not seen or heard anything. People were passing, dogs pissing, trees growing.

Back at the caravan, Simon sat at the table with his head in his hands, glaring at the contents of the envelope: a soggy bundle of Monopoly money.

'The bastard. The fucking bastard.'

Standing beside him with his arms dangling, Bernard was nodding in agreement, despite the fact he had no idea what to make of the morning's events. It was as though last night's dream had carried on in some jumbled way, as mysterious and unfathomable as the deep sea. There was a knock at the door. Bernard halted his mechanical head movement and went to answer it. The faces of Fiona and Violette appeared, haloed in the late-morning sunlight.

'Morning! Did you sleep well?'

Bernard made a face that could have passed for a smile. Simon did not look up.

'I was thinking, if you're still around at lunchtime we could have a barbecue. We've got everything we need in the caravan, even the charcoal,' said Fiona.

Bernard turned nervously to Simon and addressed his hunched back.

'Monsieur Marechall?'

'Piss off, the lot of you.'

'OK, Monsieur Marechall. I'll be right next door if you need me.'

'Get lost!'

This was not the first time he had been screwed over, but because this contract was to be the last of his long career, it left an especially bitter taste in his mouth. And it was all down to that pathetic little insurance salesman wanting to pull a fast one. He squeezed the stack of notes and a few drops of greenish liquid oozed out. No one really went out with a bang. No one. But to end up on a campsite in Cap d'Agde, escorted by a simpleton whose only wish was to play happy families, barbecuing sausages on the beach? It was a complete joke. He was going to make J.-P. Bornay swallow this Monopoly money; he would shove the whole lot down his throat!

Yet all his rage and wounded pride could not propel his spent body into action. It was all he could do to heave his leaden arse off his chair and collapse on the bed, arms outstretched. 'Poor old thing. You're worn out, like your dad's old pants. You've got plenty of money put away. As for Bornay, you win some, you lose some – what the hell does it matter? Let it go. You've had a hectic life, it's time to calm down and enjoy a peaceful old age.'

Simon clamped his hands over his ears, closed his eyes and clenched his teeth.

The face of Negrita rum, a laughing West Indian woman, came in and out of view as the bottle rolled across the floor. Once it had come to a stop against the skirting board, only her gold hoop earring was visible on the label. The last dregs of rum ran back and forth from the bottom of the bottle to the neck. Lying sprawled on the sofa, Anaïs followed the liquid's ebb and flow with bleary eyes. The bottle had slipped from her hands as she raised it to her mouth.

'Who cares, I've got another one.'

The trouble was that in order to fetch it, Anaïs would have had to get up, go into the kitchen and bend down to open the cupboard under the sink, which was all too much for her now. Everything seemed out of reach. The world was shrinking a little further from her each day. She might not have a phone, but that dolt Bernard could still get in touch. He knew how to get hold of her; he just had to give her neighbour, Fanny, a ring ... But no! He would leave his poor mother to die like a dog while he had a ball with that fancy friend of his! Well, they could all go to hell, the whole damn lot of them!

'What do you think you're looking at with those dead eyes, you stupid cow?'

The Negress went on stoically shining her sixty-watt light beneath the dusty raffia shade. She had seen all this many times before – around seven o'clock most evenings in fact.

'One day I'll drop dead and then you'll all be sorry! "Ooh, where's Anaïs? Where is she?" Well, Anaïs won't be around any more. So long, suckers! No one left to give a shit about your stupid games and dirty tricks! I'll be up there, on high, in the great big empty hole where the Good Lord's supposed to be, and I'll sit there on that old bastard's throne and I'll be the one in charge – God knows I couldn't do a worse job than him! I'll be the one laughing then, when I'm pulling all the strings, ha! No, actually, actually I'll drop everything. I'll make feathered hats for the angels and if they won't wear them, I'll send them to hell and roast them like chickens! Round and round I'll turn that spit, round and round ...'

She was rotating her right arm so enthusiastically that she fell off the sofa.

'Shit, I've hurt myself!'

An unfamiliar crowd of microscopic creatures gathered around her body, like the Lilliputians surrounding Gulliver, a motley crew of nature's embryonic creatures and freakish prototypes, too insignificant to be named. All seemed as taken aback as she was at the encounter.

'It's funny, you think you're on your own, and then ...'

Anaïs fell asleep, a beached whale snoring in a miniature world known only to alcoholics and saints.

The merguez were curling up on the barbecue, oozing a rust-coloured oil that made the coals flare up. Fiona was turning the sausages with a long-handled fork, leaning back and shielding her eyes from the smoke.

'You know, that Monsieur Marechall of yours doesn't only kill cockroaches.'

Bernard was absently bouncing Violette up and down on his knee. He had not touched the glass of rosé Fiona had just poured him. It had been difficult to give her a chronological account of the morning's events. Everything was so mixed up, his dream, the aquarium, the man dying amid the piranhas, the Monopoly money ... He could not make head nor tail of any of it. In the space of forty-eight hours he had been catapulted into another universe in which only Violette and Fiona seemed real. He clung to them like a shipwrecked man to a life raft.

'Cut some bread, will you? The guy's a professional, a

hit man, like in the movies. Except this isn't a movie,' added Fiona.

Bernard could not take his eyes off the sharp knife Fiona was using to slice the tomatoes into perfectly even rounds. He had never imagined life could be so fraught with danger. He held Violette tightly. Her vulnerability made him feel safe and he never wanted to let her go. She was his shield, his lucky charm.

Violette wriggled about in her nappy, her eyes, mouth, nose, ears and every pore of her skin wide open to each new sensation, which she recorded like a human computer. She was not thinking about anything, imagining anything or asking herself any questions and consequently did not waste time looking for answers. She was happy just to wave her arms and legs about like a beetle on its back. Staying alive was all that mattered. There was the sky, the sun and the sea, and that was enough. Her avid pupils took in all the essential details. She also knew how to shit and piss, which she duly demonstrated to stop the knee she was sitting on from jiggling.

'Fiona? I think she needs changing.'

'Again? Can you watch the merguez?'

Mother and child disappeared inside the caravan. Bernard turned over some of the sausages, which were already burnt to a cinder. The wind had picked up enough to make two or three multicoloured kites twirl gently in the sky. A black dog ran after them, barking. Between the sky and the water, the horizon stretched wide as a taut rubber band.

'One of these days it's going to snap.'

'Bernard!'

'Ah, Monsieur Marechall, are you feeling better?'

He looked like a scorched tree rooted in the sand, against a clear blue sky of the type usually found only in travel brochures.

'We're going.'

Bernard finished swallowing his mouthful of merguez sandwich.

'Are you sure you don't want something to eat before—'

'We're going.'

'OK, Monsieur Marechall, I just have to grab my jacket.'

Fiona was looking daggers at Simon. Violette was asleep on her chest, her mouth hanging open.

'It's not nice, what you're doing. Not nice at all.'

'No one asked your opinion.'

'Well, I'm giving it anyway! You'll be dead soon but you're too shit scared to go on your own. Why can't you just leave Bernard be?'

Simon did not answer. He was gazing at the sea. There was no land in sight, not even the tiniest island. Bernard came running out, putting his jacket on as he went. He looked like a kind of cormorant, clumsily gearing up for its first flight.

The interior of the car smelt of sand, salt, curdled milk and baby wee.

'You stink of piss.'

'I know, it was Violette. Shall I wind down the window? Oh, and where are we going?'

'I'll tell you.'

The traffic was moving easily as they drove along roads with curious names: Gingembre, Estragon, Genièvre, Cannelle, Place du Volcan, Passage du Thym and Passage de l'Origan, Rue des Anciens-Combattants-de-l'Afrique, Rue de la Marne, Rue du Chemin-des-Dames and finally, after Carrefour du Souvenir-Français, Rue du Rêve.

'Stop here.'

Outside number 12, a nondescript-looking man was loading suitcases into the boot of a dark-blue Audi. A tall, horsey blonde woman stood perched on her high heels, craning her neck anxiously about her.

'Now, Bernard, you're going to get out and ask them the way to Rue Jean-Mermoz.'

'Rue Jean-Mermoz, OK. Then what?'

'Then you leave me to do the rest. That's it.'

'That's it?'

'Go on, then. Take the map – make it look as though you're lost.'

The closer Bernard got to the couple, the more it felt as if he was walking the wrong way up an escalator. The short distance between them seemed to go on for ever.

'Excuse me, I'm lost. I'm looking for Rue Jean-Mermoz.'

The man was sweating. There were dark patches under the arms of his short-sleeved shirt and his balding head shone like a polished banister knob.

'Don't know it. Haven't got time.'

'But it's somewhere near here, if you look on the map ...'

The man examined the map with eyes like round marbles. The tall, horsey woman trotted over.

'I know where it is. Go back the way you came, then take—'

She didn't manage to finish her sentence. The barrel, fitted with a silencer, made a little *plop!* sound and she fell to the ground like a tree trunk sawn off at the base. Simon aimed his gun at the domed forehead of the short moustachioed man.

'On your knees. Open your mouth.'

J.-P. Bornay obeyed – or rather, his body did, and a tiny bit of his brain. As for the rest, the lights were out and there was nobody home. Everything had happened so quickly, he was beyond fear. Simon took a handful of Monopoly money out of his pocket and stuffed the notes between Bornay's teeth.

'Eat them! I said eat them!'

He began chewing slowly, wild-eyed. The map slipped from Bernard's hands and came to rest against the railings of a large house.

'You're a fool, Bornay.'

Plop! A dark hole opened up in the brow of the kneeling man and his eyes glazed over with the vague stare of a newborn baby. As he fell forwards, Simon kicked him back.

'It's done. Let's get out of here.'

Bernard would have liked nothing better than to get out of there, but his feet seemed to have sunk into the tarmac.

'Are you coming or what?'

'Monsieur Marechall ... I've shat myself ...'

'Fiona will sort it out.'

Simon got behind the wheel, since Bernard was not in a fit state. He drove cautiously, obeying stop signs and red lights.

'I feel like a glass of Suze. Do you?'

'No.'

'Wait for me out here then.'

Bernard did not feel like anything. He was as numb as a slab of frozen fish. His soiled underpants were stuck to his buttocks but he felt neither shame nor discomfort. He could have stayed like this for hours, days, years, thinking of nothing at all, oblivious to everyday life marching by on the other side of the windscreen, left, right, left, right ...

Simon downed his Suze at the counter of Bar de l'Espoir. The bar's name made him think: What was the use of hope, anyway? It served no more purpose than what he had just done, but that was simply the way it was and you had to live with it. Every time he ran out of arguments, as happened often, his father would hurl this maxim at him. It was straightforward, no-nonsense, to the point; a kind of magic formula.

The sand castle Fiona had built for Violette was quite special, with four turrets, a curved doorway and a winding road leading up to it. But the waves had already started to gnaw away at its foundations. Just her luck: clever Mummy, she'll put it back together again. The sea is mean. It draws you in, withdraws and then, as soon as you turn your back to it, comes and snatches back everything it just gave you. So much for Mother Nature. Fiona's mother, on the other hand, had been more straight with her; all she had ever given her was a childhood in care and her first name. It wasn't so bad, her name. Everyone had called her 'Fion' when she was a kid. When she turned eighteen, she had tried to find her mother but it was complicated; there was a ton of paperwork to fill in. She gave up. She thought about going on one of those TV shows that reunites long-lost relatives, but what would have been the point? What would they have had to say to each other? And so she'd got pregnant with Violette by the first guy who had happened along. All that mattered now was the two of them together, four arms, four legs, two heads. As long as they had each other, they had twice the chances of getting by. Battered by the waves with their lace of foam, one of the turrets collapsed.

The only sun on Violette was a single ray which scorched the end of her nose, in spite of the hat Fiona had made her out of the newspaper. If Violette had been able to read the article hanging over her left eye, she would have learnt that the man known as 'The Butcher of the Ardèche' had just been arrested. Though come to think of it, she probably would not have cared a jot. The only things she was interested in were her wiggly toes. When she could finally reach them, she would be a big girl.

'Anaïs, can you hear me? Georges, I think we should get her to hospital.'

The word 'hospital' was banned under Anaïs's roof, a taboo subject never to be mentioned. No sound came out of her mouth but she began rolling her eyes wildly while wringing Fanny's wrist. She was no longer averse to the idea of kicking the bucket, but it had to be in her own home. It was ashes to ashes, dust to dust – and there was no shortage of that here. The feather duster would just have to wait.

'At least go and get the doctor! Don't just stand there!'

Georges had made love to Anaïs once, a long, long time ago. Back then, Anaïs was what was known as 'a fine specimen of a woman'. This was in the days between the dirty ginger dyke running off and the dogs coming along. Fanny had gone to stay with her sister in Montélimar for a couple of days, he couldn't remember what for – a new baby, was it? Or a funeral? Anaïs had read his fortune with tarot cards ... No, actually it was some Chinese thing, I Ching. She used these wooden sticks and read baffling stuff out of a fat yellow book, like 'to retire is favourable'. In those days, retirement was the last thing on his mind: he only had eyes for those two big breasts resting on the open book, which he wanted to grab with both hands and bury his face between. The future mattered to him only when placing bets. He had opened another bottle of wine and they had rolled about on the sofa, which squeaked even then. It was over quickly, but it was good. They parted on friendly terms and it never happened again.

'What the hell are you waiting for, Georges? Can't you see she's gone blue!'

Georges left the house. He passed Jean Ferrat outside the bakery.

By the time Fiona had taken care of his clothes, Bernard had stepped back into his old skin, but not his old life. Nothing would ever be the same again. While Monsieur Marechall slept in the caravan, Bernard went for a walk on the beach with Violette nestling against his shoulder. He walked a certain distance before turning round and going back, over and over again. It was not the same sky above him now, nor the same sea. Everything had changed, but no one else had noticed. It all had the whiff of an illusion, an artful fake. Nothing was certain any more. The rocks could be made of cardboard, the pine trees out of balsa wood; Violette might be nothing but an inflatable toy, the sun a spotlight and himself just another walk-on actor. Life had lost its substance. All it had taken was a little *plop!* for everything to vanish, without explanation.

There was a small souvenir shop selling postcards next to the campsite reception. Having promised to send one to his mother, Bernard paid it a visit. The postcard he chose depicted a sunset so dazzling he almost needed sunglasses to look at it. He sat at a table in the adjoining bar and ordered a mint cordial. Violette was still asleep, glued to him like a leech. He could not think what to write, so he began with the address, chewing the cap of his pen while he waited for inspiration.

'Dear Mother ... [Was she really that dear to him?] I'm down at Cap d'Agde which is ... an up-and-down sort of place. ['Up-and-down sort of place' didn't really mean anything, and yet it summed it up perfectly. You could go from heaven to hell here and not even notice.] The weather is good. It's nice to see the sea, which is bigger than Lake Geneva.'

Bernard put down his pen and drank half his glass of mint cordial. The ice cubes had melted to the size of cuff-links. The sight of the green syrup took him back to the aquarium and made him gag. The little girl started to wriggle, dribbling into the neck of his T-shirt. Instinctively he jiggled her up and down, which made his writing wobbly.

'The sea isn't green here, same as the Red Sea isn't red. Monsieur Marechall told me that, because he's been there. It just shows you shouldn't believe everything you hear.'

Bernard drained the last drops of his drink. The ice had completely melted. He had nothing else to say so he rounded off with: 'I'm fine and hope you are too. Lots of love, your son Bernard.'

A rush of sadness surged from his chest to his eyes. He would have liked to send his mother a message in a bottle, saying: 'Come and get me, Mummy, it's too grown-up here!' But it would never arrive. He stuck on a stamp and slipped the postcard into the back pocket of his jeans.

'What a lovely baby! Is it a little boy or a little girl?'

'A little girl.'

Sitting at the next table was a podgy woman, with a mass of curly hair like a panful of macaroni. She looked like a cartoon fairy godmother.

'What's her name?'

'Violette.'

'Violette! It's good luck to be named after a flower, you know. My name's Rose.'

And she really was rosy, everything from her skin to her clothes, but not her eyes, which were periwinkle blue. She looked well over fifty and was drinking a strawberry milkshake.

'Are you here on holiday?' she asked.

'Yes and no, a bit of both.'

'I've been coming for years, same weeks, same bungalow. I'm a creature of habit. I'm from Namur, in Belgium. And you?'

'Lyon.'

'Thank heavens for that! I'm not keen on Parisians, they're so snooty! Are you having a nice time?'

'It's OK.'

'You must be here with your wife?'

'Um ... yes, but my boss as well. My wife's at the dry cleaner's and my boss is having a lie-down.'

'I see ... You must think me awfully nosy, but what do you do for a living?'

'Driver.'

'How wonderful! You must travel a lot. I'm a taxidermist.

117

Well, I'm retired now, I just do it for fun.'

'Taxi— So a bit like me, then?'

'Oh, no! I'm a taxidermist, I preserve dead animals.'

'Ah, you stuff things?'

'That's it. I used to work for museums, now I have private clients, mostly old ladies who can't bear to be parted from dead pets – dogs, cats, parrots, all sorts. Last time it was a boa constrictor!'

'A boa, really ... My boss works in a similar field, although he doesn't do preserving. He's a pest controller; he gets rid of cockroaches, bugs, mice, rats ...'

'I've done rats too! How fascinating, I'd like to meet him!'

'We're leaving tomorrow.'

'Oh, what a shame! Well, how about this evening? Come for a drink at my bungalow. It's the last one, over there, under the big pine tree.'

'I'll have to ask him ...'

'Yes, of course. I'm sure he'll agree to it. I'll expect you around seven.'

Rose was barely taller standing than she was sitting down. She called over the waiter.

'Gégé, put these two drinks on my tab, would you? So I'll see you this evening, Monsieur ...?'

'Bernard.'

She stroked Violette's cheek with her chubby little finger.

'Isn't she pretty? What lovely soft skin! And those great big eyelashes, they're like butterfly wings! You just don't want them to grow up, do you?'

She bounced off down the road like a tennis ball, the net of darkness already closing in around the trees.

Simon was well practised in taking his gun apart and putting it back together with his eyes shut. But this time he had dropped a spring and could not find it anywhere, even with his glasses on.

'Have you lost something, Monsieur Marechall?'

Bernard was standing in the hallway, his suit hanging over his arm in its plastic bag like a sheath of dead skin.

'No, I'm looking for four-leafed clover. One of the springs fell out, a stupid little spring!'

Bernard crouched down next to him and held up the missing piece.

'This one?'

'Where on earth have you been?'

'Just hanging around, waiting for Fiona to bring back my clothes.'

'We're leaving tomorrow.'

'I thought so. We haven't been here long.'

'Long enough. Help me up.'

Once he had settled back into his chair, Simon continued putting together the pieces of his deadly jigsaw puzzle. One by one he got the action working, loaded another round of bullets and secured the safety catch. His hands were shaking uncontrollably, governed by a force stronger than his own will. He clasped them tightly together, interlocking his fingers until they turned white. Bernard sat down opposite him at the table.

'I know what you really do for a living now.'

'So?'

'So nothing. It's not exactly your average nine to five.'

'The job needs doing, as long as there's a demand for it.'

'Even so, I'd have rather you just got rid of rats.'

'Rats, people – they're all the same. They breed just as quickly.'

Bernard was staring at the pistol on the table. It was hard to believe such an ordinary-looking object could do so much damage.

'Why the woman? She hadn't done anything to you.'

'No witnesses. Never leave any witnesses.'

'What about me?'

'You? Well, you're working for me, which makes you my accomplice.'

'Don't worry, I won't say a thing. I'd forget the whole thing ever happened if I could.'

'That's exactly what you have to do. Tomorrow's another day, after all.'

'Yes, and it's when we're leaving ... Oh, I met a woman earlier who does a similar sort of job to you.'

'What woman? What does she do?'

'Hang on, let me think ... Taxi-something ... She stuffs things.'

'Taxidermist?'

'That's the one! She stuffs dogs, cats, boa constrictors, all kinds of dead animals. She's Belgian and she's retired. She invited us to pop round for a drink this evening.'

Simon stood up, rubbing his back. He had to stop himself laughing. This young imbecile was really too much – first the teenage mother, now a Belgian taxidermist!

'Where on earth do you find them?'

'I didn't go out looking for her! She was the one who started talking to me. I was writing a postcard to my mother in the bar by reception. I had Violette on my lap; she was cooing over her and started chatting to me. She's here on holiday, staying in the last bungalow along the main path. Rose, her name is. She's getting on but she's got all her bits in the right places. She's expecting us at seven, but I can call it off if you'd rather.'

Simon could not help but admire Bernard's ability to adapt to the most bizarre situations. That great twerp had a born gift for resilience.

'Well, why not?'

'I was worried you'd be angry. Right, I'd better go and tell Fiona – I didn't want to say anything before talking to you ... Oh and by the way, she thinks Fiona and I are married and Violette's our daughter. I couldn't put her straight, it would have got too complicated.'

'And I'm the granddad, am I?'

'No! You're my boss, I'm your driver.'

'Well, that's all right then. OK, off you go, back to your little family.'

Simon could not remember the last time he had been in such a good mood. He smiled as he weighed the gun in his hand, the steel gradually warming in his palm. It was nothing but a memento now, like the tools retired labourers hold on to as a reminder of times gone by. They had come a long way together, he and his gun, but neither seemed fit for much any more. He slid it under his pillow out of habit, but something told him he would not be using it again and he felt a huge weight lifting.

Rose had everything she could possibly need in her bungalow, with glasses for every type of drink and a crocheted coaster to go under each one. Olives, peanuts, cocktail sausages and homemade crisps were piled high in cut-glass dishes. The hostess twirled around the table in a flimsy lilac chiffon negligee like a moth dancing in the light of the scented anti-mosquito lamp. She had a kind word for everyone, especially Violette, whose cheek she stroked each time she went past. Simon and Fiona were on the pastis, Rose on beer, Bernard on mint cordial and Violette on her bottle, staring up at Venus in the night sky. Unlike her neighbours, Rose had personalised her bungalow, decorating it with fairy lights, frilly curtains and pots of brightly coloured geraniums.

'It's another place to call my own. I've been coming here for so long, the same weeks every year. Francis, the manager, gets everything ready for me before I arrive. It's like having a second home, I suppose. I like to feel at home wherever I am.

The world belongs to all of us, doesn't it?'

'Absolutely!'

'Namur is a pretty little town but the winter goes on for ever! Do you know Namur, Monsieur Marechall?'

'Yes. I'm from the north, so Belgium's just across ... We used to go over to buy beer and tobacco. But I haven't been back in a long time.'

'It's pretty much the same. The north will never change. And what about you, Madame Fiona, where are you from?'

'From a care home. Don't s'pose it's changed much there either. My mother was Italian, I think, or maybe it was my dad ... You have to make these things up, when you don't know the truth.'

'Of course you do, my poor darling ... Well, you have your own family now. All that matters is the here and now.'

'That's right. Excuse me for a moment, I need to go and change the baby.'

'Be my guest!'

'Will you give me a hand, Bernard?'

Simon and Rose watched the young couple and their baby disappearing into the shadows. The image was almost biblical.

'How wonderful to be young!'

'Indeed!'

'Can I get you another?'

'Just a drop.'

There was a bit of peanut stuck between Simon's teeth.

He tried to dislodge it with the tip of his tongue, but there was no shifting it. Soon he could concentrate on nothing else.

'So you get rid of rodents, I hear?'

'Not just rodents, all kinds of pests. But I've just sold my company to take retirement.'

'You'll never look back! To begin with you won't know what to do with yourself, but really you won't have a care in the world ... unless you worry about how long you've got left.'

'I don't think about it.'

'Oh, I do. I don't have a problem with dying, it's eternity I'm worried about. The first animal I preserved was a squirrel. Poor little thing! If you'd seen the state he was in ... a truck had run him over. But now he's fresh as the day he was born! You'll think me ridiculous, but I feel like ... like I'm giving the Creator a helping hand, fixing His mistakes. Plus I enjoy needlework.'

'Nothing wrong with that. I've got nothing against eternity, but personally I think I'd die of boredom.'

'Ah, come on, you'd get used to it eventually!'

Rose looked like a Chinese lantern. Her chubby face bobbed from side to side and her wide smile revealed all her teeth, no doubt just as false as the pearls she wore around her neck. Was falseness really the enemy of truth? Rose reminded him of the Hanoi madam who was just as happy to pocket fake dollars as real ones. Their hands were lying on the table millimetres apart. She was not wearing a wedding ring, and neither was he.

'It's getting chilly, I think I'll put a shawl on.'

Simon lit a cigarette. Without meaning to, he blew a smoke

ring that settled around his head like a halo. Meanwhile, in her largest saucepan, the Great Bear was cooking up a fricassee of stars.

'Didn't you see the way she was touching her?'

'She likes children.'

'Of course she does, she's a witch! She can do what she likes with her stuffed goats, but I don't want her coming anywhere near Violette.'

'Fiona! You're going a bit far, she's just a little old lady—'

'I don't like old people! They stink, that's why they put on so much perfume. They're all at death's door, just like your precious Monsieur Marechall!'

The nappy spread with innocent shit fell into the bin with a dull thud. Violette was lying on her back, squirming and whimpering.

'You don't think you're being a teensy bit paranoid?'

'Of course I am! That's the reason I'm still alive today. Your boss is a hit man, Rose is a monster, and you ... you're just a stupid idiot!'

She threw herself into Bernard's arms, sobbing and pounding his back with her fists.

'Let's get out of here, you, me and Violette. I don't want us to be tainted by them. We have a right to live our lives, damn it!'

Fiona was wearing a new face. The tears streaming down it gave it the appearance of an unfinished watercolour, an island emerging from the mist.

127

'Make love to me.'

'What here? Now?'

'Yes.'

Not easy, no, it was not easy at all, but when Violette's right hand managed to grab her left big toe, she was over the moon. She had finally caught the stupid thing and now she was going to stuff it in her mouth. That was it: she was a big girl now.

'We need to get you to hospital, Anaïs. Believe me, I know what I'm talking about. This is a matter of life or death.'

'Who the hell do you think you are? Already dead, are you? Know all about it, huh? No? Well then, shut your trap.'

She did not actually say this to the doctor since her jaws refused to come unstuck, but by God she had thought it. A needle had just pricked her arm, spreading its welcome venom through her body. Fanny and the doctor were talking in hushed tones in the corner. From time to time, Fanny lifted her arms and let them drop again in a symbol of helplessness, like a fledgling bird afraid to fly the nest. Georges stood with his hands clasped behind his back, in conversation with the Negress lamp. Why couldn't they all just go away and leave her alone? ... Things were going just as well for Anaïs as for the rest of them, better even, since she did not intend to carry on any longer. She just had to wait for them to get fed up and piss off. She was used to waiting, she had been doing it all her

life – hanging around for buses, love, success, a phone call
... Strangely, the less time she had left, the less the waiting
bothered her.

The doctor was the first to leave the scene, carrying his little
bag filled with needles, rubber tubes, pills and bottles. Then
it was the turn of Georges, whose lumbering uselessness was
beginning to get on his wife's nerves. He did not wait to be told
twice. Death, like birth, was not a sight he was madly keen to
see. He was happy enough to stick where he was, somewhere
between the two. Fanny, on the other hand, settled into the
armchair next to the sofa where Anaïs lay, determined to watch
over her, offering her puny body as a shield against all harm.
It was a laudable stance, but within quarter of an hour she was
snoring, her chin resting on her bony chest. Anaïs coughed
and shifted until she was sure her neighbour's nasal symphony
was in full swing, before sitting herself up. It was a struggle,
but she made it. Her head was spinning, but what did it matter?
She had got her sea legs years ago. The pains running from
shoulder to hip did not bother her any more. She had adopted
them and tamed them, like mangy stray cats. Having reached
the edge of the sofa, she attempted to stand, only to discover
this was a risky enterprise. Crawling on all fours, she moved
towards the kitchen. It was a tricky business, but more stable
than relying on her hind legs. Besides, this was how everyone
took their first steps and learnt to be independent. She just had
to throw herself back in time, to the days of discovering the
world from the ground up. Right arm ... Left knee ... Left arm
... Right knee.

Once again, the parallel world of miniature creatures shyly gathered to spur her on. She knew she could trust the little monsters, because they were cute. They bent over backwards to help her push open the kitchen door. The floor was icy cold, each tile a territory to be conquered. With the effort of crossing it, she blew powerful gusts from her nose and mouth which scattered the flocks of grey fluff and whipped up crumbs, like an elephant stomping through the undergrowth. Anaïs came to a halt in front of the cupboard under the sink, where normal people keep their cleaning products and alcoholics keep their bottles. The last bottle of Negrita was definitely in there somewhere, but where ...?

It was pitch black inside the cupboard. Anaïs groped about blindly, picking out various plastic and glass containers by touch. But danger was lurking in the absurd habit she had picked up from her mother – a house-proud woman of strict morals – of pouring the last drops of detergents, bleach and the like into empty bottles to save space. Since at Anaïs's house the only empties were Negrita bottles, and on top of that she could not see a thing, the whole operation was very likely to end in disaster. But she was so thirsty! All around her the little creatures held their breath.

'Now let's see if God exists!'

She grabbed the first bottle at random and took a long swig.

Simon pushed away the flabby thigh resting on top of his and freed himself from the tangle of sheets. He felt sick. The heady smell of Rose's perfume was overpowering. Unless it was something else, a deeper disgust at an entire existence, which rose in his throat, mingled with the aftertaste of pastis. Walking on tiptoe, he gathered his belongings and left the bungalow. The cool night air did him good but not enough to stop him emptying his stomach, clutching the rough trunk of a pine tree with both hands. He got dressed, shivering from head to foot. He had not been able to do it. 'It doesn't matter,' she had whispered in his ear, 'at our age ...'

Apart from a window at reception and a few street lamps along the main path, there were no lights on. It was like a graveyard. The regular ebb and flow of the waves made the dreary walk seem to go on for ever. When he finally reached his caravan, the car that should have been parked next to it was gone.

'The little bastard!'

Bernard's bed had not been slept in. Simon ran back out to Fiona's caravan. Deserted. He was seized with a strange panic, as though he had died and no one had thought to tell him. Even solitude, his only companion for as many years as he could remember, seemed to have let go of his hand. The darkness was becoming denser around him, invading his nose, mouth and ears like the soot of his childhood. He staggered back to his caravan, turned on all the lights and searched under his pillow. The gun was there, warmed by the cushions but utterly useless. He sat on the edge of the bed, the weapon dangling between his thighs like a flaccid penis, staring past the half-open door into a picture of crushing emptiness. He had been scared many times before, but never like this. This was a childlike, uncontrollable fear that was slowly shutting him down like an anaesthetic. 'Be still my beating heart.' He felt neither hate nor anger, he just could not understand.

'Why have you done this to me, kid? Why?'

A chemical precipitation, caused by a complex mixture of conflicting emotions, made a warm, salty liquid spring from the corner of his eyes, a liquid he had not tasted for what seemed like centuries. The teardrop trickled through the network of lines on his cheek to the corner of his mouth, and from his lips to his chin. It felt as good and sweet as an endless ejaculation. For once, his heart was doing more than pumping blood around his body. He raised himself up painlessly, walked towards the beach, crossed the strip of grey sand and immersed himself up to the waist in the black waters. And there, swinging his arm like a farmer sowing seeds, he tossed the gun as far as he could throw it. The weapon went to join the pile of junk that carpets the sea bed, just another thing among all the others, just as Simon was only one among many humans.

'Don't you think we might be doing something really, really stupid?'

'What are you talking about? Surely you don't actually think your Monsieur Marechall's going to shop us to the police?'

'No, not that ...'

'Well, what then? Where do you think you were going with him? Straight into a brick wall, that's where, or else going inside. And as for that old hag, she'd have had Violette off me and stuffed her, no question.'

'That's total rubbish! What the hell are we going to do in Spain? I can't speak a word of Spanish.'

'It's no harder than Italian. In Italian, you put an "i" on the end of every word and in Spanish you put an "o". Also Spain's really close and I've got friends in Barcelona.'

'Really?'

'Well, acquaintances, but that'll do, right? We deserve another shot at life. You have to take your chances where you find them.'

'I suppose ...'

Fiona was sitting in the back, with Violette sprawled across her lap. Looking at her in the rear-view mirror, Bernard saw the face of a stubborn little girl, closed like a fist. How could people change so quickly? Last night, in the half-light of the caravan, she had seemed so gentle, or at least so calm, like Violette after a feed. They had made love with the lightness of two butterflies, simply, without haste or hunger. She had fallen asleep, or perhaps just closed her eyes. She was breathing in time with the child asleep in the Moses basket, following the rhythm of the night. The beauty spot on her left breast was the centre of a world in which pain, fear and sadness were no more. Bernard held his breath, for fear of bursting the fragile bubble in which they were floating. Never before had he felt so complete, a man in perfect harmony with his life. He was exactly where he should be. Then she had opened her eyes so suddenly, he was startled.

'Let's get out of here, Bernard!'

'Uh, where to?'

'Spain.'

'Spain? When?'

'Straight away, right now, this minute.'

Even the sky looked different today. Milky clouds trailed across a sun as ill-disposed as Bernard to starting the new day. The landscape seemed dull and flat, patches of land blistered with characterless houses.

'I'll have to stop and get petrol.'

'OK, I'll sort Violette out.'

They stopped at a service station selling any old rubbish at any price to anyone who would buy it. As he paid for his tank of petrol, Bernard noted bitterly that they were getting through money like there was no tomorrow. They were running low already and by the time they got to Barcelona there would be nothing left. Spain, for goodness' sake! The petrol station was already trying to flog plastic bulls, castanets and models of gleaming toreadors and flouncy flamenco dancers. They had not yet crossed the border and already he felt homesick. But what was troubling him most was the dirty trick they had played on Monsieur Marechall. OK, he was a hit man, a criminal, but he was much more than that. Monsieur Marechall had always been straight down the line with him and had put his trust in Bernard. He had taught him things like ... that the Red Sea isn't red, for one. He had treated him like a man, like a son almost, and he, eight-fingered Bernard, had behaved like the lowest of the low, nothing but a common thief. His reflection in the window disgusted him. He would never be able to look himself in the eye again. He was worth less than a cigarette butt in an ashtray.

Fiona reappeared, spruced up. She had caught the sun on her nose and cheeks, which made her look like a shiny little toffee apple.

'They're selling car seats for babies in there – what do you think? It would make things a lot easier. I've had enough of sitting there with Violette plonked in my lap. What's the matter? What's that face for?'

'Listen, I'm not going any further, Fiona. Here, take what's left of the money and you go to Barcelona, but I'm taking the car back to Monsieur Marechall.'

'Are you out of your mind? We're almost at the border — we'll be in Barcelona by this evening!'

'I couldn't care less about Spain. I've never cheated anybody and I can't do it, I just can't do it.'

One big, tight ball of words was stuck in Fiona's throat, which she could not spit out or swallow. She was choking and looking helplessly about her. All around people were getting into their cars, munching snack bars and holding paper cups. Others were getting out, stretching their legs with hands on hips, walking their dogs or scolding snivelling kids ... Normal people.

'Christ, Bernard! Look around you. Don't you want to be happy? Don't you want an easy life like all these people have? You and me, we met each other and that means something. We can have a life of our own, just us, like we've never had before. We have a right to that, damn it! We deserve it!'

'I want that too, Fiona, it's all I want. But I can't do it by going behind someone's back. I couldn't look at myself in the mirror again.'

'But he doesn't give a shit about you, your Monsieur Marechall! He's using you, and once he's got what he wants from you he'll put a bullet through your head.'

'I don't think so, Fiona, I don't believe that. Listen, here's what we're going to do. You take the money and go to Barcelona to stay with your friends. I'll take the car back and then I'll come and meet you there. I promise you, I swear.'

'I don't know if you're just stupid or completely naïve, or both. You're leaving us here in a fucking service station car park to go back to a murdering old bastard, and you're telling me you can't bear to let somebody down? What kind of an idiot do you take me for? It would be funny if it wasn't so pathetic!'

Fiona sat down on a low concrete wall, her eyes brimming with tears. Violette started to whimper, then cry.

'Oh, don't you start!'

'Calm down, Fiona. Don't talk to her like that. Give her to me.'

'NO! Don't you touch her! Go on, fuck off! Get out of here! I don't want your fucking loot! I'm telling you, get the hell away from me!'

People were turning to look at them. Bernard crouched down in front of the girls with his head in his hands and his back bent. Why did life have to give with one hand and take away with the other?

'They seemed like such a nice couple as well. Are you going to report them?'

'I don't think so.'

'They looked as though butter wouldn't melt though, didn't they? It makes you wonder if you can trust anyone ... You know, I saw that man on the news the other day, the one who killed the three English girls, being taken into court by two policemen. Believe it or not, they were the ones who looked dodgy. The killer just looked like your average man in the street, like you or me.'

Simon was stroking the sand with the flat of his hand, making figures of eight, building little heaps and watching the grains running through his fingers. He had not moved since sunrise, having stayed up all night waiting for it. Rose had passed him on her morning jog and sat down next to him. She had not stopped to draw breath, eagerly filling every silence the way people do when visiting sick relatives. It did not bother him;

she was just another part of the scenery. The sky had clouded over and an easterly wind ruffled the crests of the waves, threw up swirls of sand and tossed light objects about.

'It's going to rain later.'

'Maybe.'

'Do you think they'll come back?'

'I don't know.'

'What will you do?'

'I haven't thought about it.'

It was true. He had not come to any decisions. He was just there, as he always had been, wherever he was in the world. He was an island.

'Don't worry, it'll sort itself out. Young people mess about but in the end ... Listen. How about I take you out for lunch?'

'That's very kind of you.'

'Great! I'll go and get changed. Come and meet me at the bungalow.'

'Will do.'

Rose bounced off along the shore like a beach ball. An injured seagull was batting one wing and emitting piercing squawks. All the other seagulls had abandoned it to its fate. Tired of flapping around, it sat on a rock and waited for a miracle that would never come. In which part of Africa was it that people greeted each other every morning with the question 'How's the pain?'

Simon could no longer remember.

'No, Marike, he's not a toy boy, he's the real deal, our sort of age. But he's a good-looking man, not an ounce of fat on him, smartly dressed, very proper ... You bet I'd like to take him back to Namur ...! He's selling his business, he's retiring ... What's he like in bed! There's more to life than that, you know ... Very affectionate, yes ... I couldn't tell you if he's been married before, I only met him yesterday ... Right, I must go, I've got to get ready, I'm taking him out for lunch. The poor thing, he had his car stolen ... That's right, Marike, I'll tell you all about it. Speak soon.'

In the bedroom of the bungalow, the mirror had given up trying to follow Rose's hour-long dance of the seven veils. A dozen dresses, each lacier than the last, were piled up on the bed. Rain began to hammer down on the roof. Rose glanced up, wincing.

Simon was sorry to leave the beach. The sand seemed to bristle with buckshot. The seagull hid its head under its good wing.

'It's the best fish restaurant in town. I can recommend the squid *à la sétoise*, it's delicious!'

After ordering, Rose slipped off to the toilet. Simon reached over to the next table and picked up the newspaper. Smiling shots of Bornay, his mistress and his wife filled the front page: 'CRIME OF PASSION OR COLD-BLOODED MURDER?' He skimmed the article. The three victims had been killed with the same weapon. Strangely enough, the same calibre of pistol had also been used in the aquarium shooting of a man with a murky past. The guard had seen two men fleeing the scene but had been unable to give detailed descriptions. It was dark, everything had happened very quickly. There was no apparent link between the two incidents.

Simon folded up the newspaper, indifferent. As far as he was concerned, it was nothing to do with him. He had always wiped the slate clean at the end of every contract, so that remorse and regret had no chance of rearing their heads. Simon was a pro, a sort of bailiff who did what he was told, no questions asked. He took lives the way others removed furniture.

The squid *à la sétoise* was indeed excellent. Rose was talking passionately about her craft, the art of preserving the appearance of life. It was a constant struggle against time, as flesh is fragile and, even treated, deteriorates quickly.

'But you can do amazing things these days! Especially with the eyes – I've got drawers full of them: dogs' eyes, cats' eyes, all kinds of birds' eyes. It's what I put on last, the cherry on the cake, if you will. The eyes are where all the life is. Take you, for example. You come across as rather hard, almost severe, but your eyes are full of tenderness, with a hint of melancholy. It's very touching. I suspect that's why you rarely take off those dark glasses, to hide any sign of weakness. Forgive me, I'm prying.'

'Nonsense!'

'I can't help myself. I just can't resist peering into people's hearts, because that's where all the mystery is, don't you think? Right there, at the heart of the heart.'

'Absolutely. But remember if you peer over too far, you might fall.'

'At my age, there's not much left to lose. You could just as easily fall in love as into a coma ...'

When Rose blushed, she glowed like hot metal. Simon felt like throwing a bucket of water over her to cool her down. She fanned herself with her napkin. They had been the first to arrive and now that they had reached dessert, the restaurant was heaving.

'It's boiling in here! Do you fancy going for a stroll? It's stopped raining.'

'I'd like that very much.'

This is what he was planning to say: 'Monsieur Marechall, I'm very sorry for what I did but, as you can see, I've brought your car back. I don't want you to think I'm some petty thief. I don't know what came over me – maybe I'm in love. Maybe I was scared, too. You have to admit you do a funny sort of job. But I do respect it, and you've always been straight with me. So if you want, I'll carry on with the job and take you back to Vals, even if you don't give me the rest of the money. You know, I just want a quiet life with Fiona and Violette, earning enough to get by. You see, I'm an honest person and I'll always have good memories of you, even if you don't want anything more to do with me. It's up to you.'

Fiona was sleeping on the back seat, or pretending to. It had been no easy matter, winning her over, but at the end of the day she had probably had enough of being shunted from pillar to post. On top of that it was raining and maybe, just maybe, she did have feelings for him, even if she had never said as much.

144

'He'll put a bullet through that thick head of yours.'

He had bought the car seat to console her. It was tricky to fit, with all its straps, buckles and hooks. The baby was bright red, strapped into the seat with her arms sticking out like two little wings. But she did not cry. Her big round eyes stared at the treetops, the roofs and the telegraph wires flashing past, outlined against the grey, rain-streaked sky. She had nothing against the car but preferred the beach because it was bigger and the things around her stayed still. When she grew up she would be a civil servant, with an office all to herself and everything neatly arranged. Every day would be like the day before. This dream of stability made her so happy that she pooed and wet herself all at once, and then blissfully wallowed in the warm, soft mulch.

God existed, but He did not look like the pissed-off Father Christmas character people usually imagined. For starters, He was a She, and She was black. She wore a madras cotton turban, two big hoop earrings, and a huge smile. She had created rum in her own image and the little creatures rejoiced at this revelation, breaking out in a frenzied Caribbean *biguine* around Anaïs.

She stood up almost effortlessly. Now if that wasn't a miracle! She took another good swig to buck herself up for her first steps into this brave new world. Then she screwed the lid back on tightly and placed the bottle on the draining board; that way she no longer ran the risk of confusing God with a common cleaning product. Thinking of cleaning, she frowned, taking in just how filthy her kitchen had become; two weeks' washing up was stacked in a perilous pyramid, the cooker was caked with grease and the lino stuck to the soles of her slippers. Feeling in great shape, she armed herself with a scourer and a floor cloth and rolled up her sleeves.

The clattering of pans roused Fanny from her sleep. She rubbed her eyes. Anaïs was not on the sofa.

'Anaïs ...? What on earth are you doing?'

'The housework, obviously. Don't come in, I'm washing the floor!'

'But what about the doctor?'

'Yes, what about the doctor?'

'You were ...'

'Well, I'm not any more – I'm on top of the world! And it's not down to that stupid so-and-so, it's thanks to God. I've just seen Him, clear as I see you now. That's right, dear, it doesn't just happen at Lourdes, you know. Now listen, Fanny, I'm very grateful for everything you've done but, as you can see, I've got my work cut out here. It's getting late and I know Georges doesn't like to be on his own at night, so please, go back and keep him company.'

'Are you sure ...?'

'Positive. Off you go.'

Fanny took herself off, shaking her head, and Anaïs turned on the radio. As luck would have it, Jean Ferrat was singing 'La Montagne'.

The kitchen was now gleaming but Anaïs wasn't done yet. She tackled the bedroom next, then the sitting room. Untouched for decades, the vacuum cleaner seemed to be enjoying its own second wind, sucking up so much dust she had to change the bag three times. She saved the Negress lamp until last, polishing every nook and cranny with a soft cloth.

'Oh, Negrita, dearest Negrita! We should bow down before you!'

It was two in the morning when Anaïs finally sank back onto the sofa, basking in the glow of her hard work.

'My God, I'm hungry. I could eat a raw elephant!'

Anaïs unearthed a tin of sardines and began devouring them, mopping up the sauce with a crust of stale bread. She had patched things up with life now; the last mouthful of rum sealed the deal. Afterwards she let out a loud burp, a delicate combination of oily fish and alcohol. She scrupulously washed her plate, glass and cutlery, brushed her teeth and went to her room, put on a pair of Japanese pyjamas she had never worn before, and slipped between the clean sheets of the freshly made bed. She was not ready to sleep, not with this feeling of serenity bathing her like amniotic fluid. In the warm glow of the bedside lamp, whose shade was draped in a pink scarf, she lay with her hands behind her head and closed her eyes, smiling like a baby.

'Now all I need is a project I can get my teeth into ...'

The pavement of Boulevard du Front-de-Mer was drying in patches. The sky looked off-colour and the sea was the shade of a dodgy oyster. The wind was doing its utmost to get inside the shawl wrapped tightly around Rose's chest.

'It's almost like being back home. The weather's always like this in Belgium, even on a good day. We're used to it, but you still get sick of it sometimes. You've travelled a lot, haven't you, Simon?'

'A fair amount.'

'To hot countries?'

'Yes. You can get sick of blue sky too.'

'What are you going to do, now you're retired?'

'Nothing, like everyone else.'

'Oh, you mustn't! You need to make plans. You could come and see me in Namur?'

'Why not ...'

Yes, why not? Rose's house was bound to be cosy. He could

sit warming his feet in front of the stove, flicking through an atlas in search of an imaginary island. Rose would cook him chicory *à la cassonade* or *au jambon*. And then he'd die and she would stuff him, putting glass eyes in his empty sockets to make him look alive. That was as good a plan as any. He was smiling to himself at the thought of it when a searing pain shot through him like a bolt of lightning. It took his breath away. All he could see were streaks and bubbles, like film melting under the heat of a projector.

'Are you OK, Simon? ... Simon!'

Luckily since the promenade was used mainly by the elderly, there was a bench every five metres. Rose sat him down, patting his hand and cheeks and saying words he could not understand.

'I'm going to get my car. We'll go back to the bungalow and I'll call a doctor. Stay where you are, I'll be right back.'

The pain had gone, leaving nothing behind but the tail of a comet thrashing in empty space. 'I'm sitting on a bench ... I'm sitting on a bench ...' was all he managed to think.

'So what does your mother sell in her shop?'

'Uh, nothing. She's had a go at selling loads of things but it never worked out. Now she just lives there, if you can call it a life. Have you seen this? Violette loves ketchup!'

The baby was greedily suckling Bernard's sauce-covered finger.

'Well done, you've got it all over her. She looks like Dracula or something.'

The snack bar where they had stopped for sausage and chips was empty apart from the owner and a guy clinging to the bar like a mussel to its bed.

'What's the point in a shop that doesn't sell anything?'

'There isn't one.'

'What's Vals like?'

'Small. It's quite smart on one side of the Volane, with the baths, casino, hotels and gardens for the old and rich. It's completely dead across the river, where the old and skint live.'

'Sounds like paradise ... you really know how to treat a girl!'

'I never said we had to stay there. It's where my mother lives, that's all.'

'Have you never thought of doing something with the shop?'

'No, like what?'

'Well, I don't know ... But in a touristy town like that, you can always sell something. Tourists get bored, so they buy stuff.'

'Hmm ... if that was true, my mother would be a millionaire by now.'

'Maybe she just hasn't found the right thing yet.'

'Maybe.'

On the other side of the steamed-up window, cars were driving up and down the road like grey ghosts. On their plates, the few leftover crooked chips were returning to the frozen state the cook had briefly released them from, floating in a swamp of ketchup. Fiona was puffing on a cigarette and daydreaming, resting her cheek on her hand. Bernard was cradling the little monster snoring through her wrinkled-up nose.

'How big's this shop?'

'About half the size of this place, I'd say, maybe a bit smaller. And it's a bit of a mess. Well, it's falling apart.'

'But you said it's on the main road, didn't you?'

'Yes, but in the poor bit, so it might as well be a dead end. Every day except market day, it's: "Move along, nothing to see here!" Don't start getting ideas, that's what wrecked my mother's life. We can go back to Bron; there's a job waiting for me up there. The streets aren't exactly paved with gold, but it's steady money.'

'I'm not getting ideas. I'm just interested, that's all.'

'Anyway, once you've seen it you'll know exactly what I mean. Shall we get going?'

Violette agreed to be strapped in without protest, one eye open, the other shut, her lips pursed in resignation. Fiona joined Bernard in the front, which made him happy. Once he had put a bit of money aside, he would buy himself a car. Nothing as flashy as Monsieur Marechall's, but his own set of wheels all the same. He already had the child seat, which was a start. Fiona put her hand on his thigh and turned on the radio. Before setting off, they kissed like kids, their mouths tasting of warm Coke and ketchup.

'Men are always the first to go, whether they run off with a tart or kick the bucket,' thought Rose. 'Marike's right, you have to get them young, at least then you have a chance of holding on to them. Not that she has it much better herself; she's still a widow with gold-diggers sniffing around her. "Stormy weather, brightening up later on," they said on the radio this morning. Fat chance!'

She was absently plaiting together the tassels of her shawl, sitting on the edge of the bed where Simon lay fully clothed but for his shoes. He had categorically refused to let her call a doctor. A handful of pills and he had fallen asleep, ashen-faced with two great purple bags under his eyes. Rose had never been married, at first because she did not believe in it – or to avoid being ditched like her mother was – and later out of habit. It was only in the last four or five years that she had begun to think about ending her days with someone – with a man, that is. She was healthy, comfortably off, had plenty to keep herself busy, but she was unable to shake off a growing sense of sadness. She had even thought about taking out a lonely hearts ad or signing up to a dating agency, but her pride had stopped her; she wanted a real love affair, the kind that comes along when you least expect it. In a sense she was already in love, but did not yet know with whom. Then this Simon chap had turned up out of nowhere! Despite having known him only twenty-four hours, she had realised straight away he was the one. And seeing him like this now, lying stiff with his hands crossed over his stomach, his nostrils pinched and skin waxy – it was too much to take in. The tricks life plays on us ...

'Shoot, Simon! Just shoot, damn it! It hurts too much, I'm finished ...'

The weapon trembled in Simon's hand, the barrel pointing at his friend Antoine's forehead. Simon had killed men before, but on the battlefield you were never quite sure – the enemy was too far away, hidden by branches and rocks. This time it was different, standing inches away from his friend's pain-racked face.

'We're all born to die ... Shoot, please!'

Simon had shut his eyes. He was a little boy, crawling under the table where his mother was shelling peas and chatting with her friends. It was dark underneath their dresses. His finger had pulled the trigger. Not him, his finger. Ever since, each time he killed a man, he saw himself back under that table, amid a forest of grey woollen-stockinged legs.

*

What was Rose doing? It looked like she was knitting. Those podgy little hands ... He held out his open palm. Rose turned to him, the lashes of her owl-like eyes caked in lumpy mascara, a weak smile on her lips.

'How are you feeling?'

'So, what did he say?'

'Nothing. He didn't even seem surprised. He just looked at me.'

After dropping Fiona and Violette at their caravan, Bernard had parked the car outside Monsieur Marechall's. He was out. Bernard had immediately thought of Rose. All the way to her bungalow, he kept running over the speech he had prepared in the car. But he got muddled, jumbling his words. By the time he knocked at the door, his mind was utterly blank. Rose let him in. Her make-up was smeared, but she was smiling. Monsieur Marechall was sitting on the edge of the bed, his hands cupping a mug of hot tea. His shoelaces were undone, his skin sallow and almost translucent, the rim of his eyes the dull pink of ham that's past its best. He looked like one of those antique Chinese ivory figurines. There was no movement to his face, no trace of emotion in his expression. Bernard felt dizzy looking at him. Eventually he managed to prise his tongue from his palate and speak.

'It's me, Monsieur Marechall. I came back. I brought the car ...'

No reaction. Total silence.

'I'm sorry, I ...'

Rose came to his rescue, placing her hand on his shoulder.

'It's OK, Bernard, leave it. Simon had a funny turn earlier on, but he's a lot better now. Don't worry. Are Fiona and the baby with you?'

'Yes.'

'Good, good. Go back and see them. I'll be along in a little while.'

As he allowed himself to be ushered out, Bernard thought he saw a smile hovering over Monsieur Marechall's lips, but perhaps that was just what he wanted to see.

'He didn't say anything at all? He didn't even call you an idiot?'

'Not a word, I swear. He was just staring at me, but at the same time I'm not sure he really saw me at all.'

'He must have been seriously shaken. I once saw a guy get an electric shock while he was fixing a meter. Christ, he looked like he'd come back from the dead! What if he pops his clogs tonight, or tomorrow? What'll we do then?'

'I don't know. Let's not think about it.'

'You really hit the jackpot with that one, I'm telling you. Anyway, we're out of milk for Violette – do you want to go and get some?'

'Anaïs? You're up?'

'Of course I am. I'm not exactly going to do my shopping on all fours!'

'I heard you were ill ...'

'Well, you heard wrong. Where's the grated Gruyère?'

'At the back, in the dairy section.'

Anaïs's bulk filled the narrow aisles as she moved up and down the shelves of the Petit Casino. Her wellingtons squeaked and her umbrella dripped, leaving a snail trail on the tiled floor. She had such good memories of the previous evening's sardines that she picked up three cans, followed by pasta, rice, flour, chocolate, biscuits, peas, eggs ... Other than the three bottles of Negrita, she grabbed products at random, not even bothering to look at what she was throwing into her basket. The truth was she couldn't care less. She just wanted to fill her cupboards, as though preparing for a siege. She only stopped stuffing things into her basket when the handle began to dig into her arm. She barely managed to haul it up to the till. After putting through all her purchases, the grocer looked less than pleased to be told she would pay him tomorrow.

'Don't you believe me?'

'Yes, but—'

'Bernard's coming back this evening, or tomorrow. He'll drop by and settle the bill.'

It was still raining, the water glazing the road and fringing the gutters. Faceless, stooped figures scurried along, keeping close to the walls. It was this rotten weather that had made Anaïs stock up, because it was going to carry on like this for ages, perhaps even until the end of the world. It made no difference to her since she was already dead, but eternity was a long time and she needed to be ready for it.

Back home, she put down her umbrella and took off her raincoat with a sigh and swapped the oversized wellington boots for her good old slippers.

'The sky can fall in if it wants. We've got everything we need, haven't we, princess?'

The Negress lamp smiled back at her. She went into the kitchen to put away her supplies, poured herself a good glass of rum and stood back to admire the cans lined up like ornaments on the shelves.

'Now, give me one good reason why I should go out. Just one!'

She started to laugh, the same laugh as the woman on the Negrita bottle.

By now Rose was treating Bernard almost as a son, asking after Fiona and the baby. She had said, 'Simon had a funny turn earlier on,' talking as though they were all part of the same family, of which he, Simon, was the head. There was something both comical and touching about it. What on earth did they have in common? When Bernard had walked in like a great sheepish oaf, Simon could not help but see in him not a physical resemblance, but a kind of unexpected extension of himself. That was why he had looked at him without speaking. It was strange. It was as if they had all been shipwrecked and fate had thrown them together on a desert island. The situation they found themselves in was so out of the ordinary it was as if their pasts no longer existed, but had gone down with the rest of humanity. They were all flailing, naked, towards one another, each seeking some comfort, some reason for their survival.

Thinking him asleep, Rose had tiptoed out, probably to go and see Fiona and the baby. Simon was still feeling weak but he could not stay in the bungalow any longer, suffocated by Rose's cloying perfume. He needed fresh air. It was hard going, walking through the wet sand. It clung to his soles like clay. As a child, he would go out and gather potatoes from the muddy fields and come home with his feet caked in muck. Sometimes you would be in it up to your knees. Every step you took, the slippery earth sucked you in further with a disgusting slurp. In Indonesia, he had seen men sink into the swamps. Once their head had disappeared, a big bubble formed on the surface of the bog, then it burst and it was all over. It would probably be his turn to go under soon. The idea itself was not so hard to stomach; what bothered him was not knowing when or where. Until now, he had always been the one to decide such things. Except with Antoine ... He remembered it like a baptism, but the other way round. That was how he wanted to go, the way Antoine had: at the hands of a friend. Simon had been around Bernard's age at the time ...

'Did you never have kids because you couldn't, Rose?'

'No. I just never found the right man.'

'But you must have been pretty once. You're not bad-looking now!'

'Thanks. I had plenty of offers, but I didn't want to be tied down. I was anxious to keep my freedom.'

'That doesn't have to stop you! Freedom means a lot to me too. But I wanted a kid of my own. So I went with the first half-decent-looking guy who came along.'

'It was a bit different in my day. And what about Bernard?'

'It's different this time. I already have Violette, for one thing. We've only just met. We'll see. If things go well with us, maybe we'll have another one together.'

Rose was tickling Violette gently. The little girl appeared to enjoy this, smiling and gurgling. Chubby girls understand each other. Fiona draped a babygro over the radiator to dry.

'You know, Rose, don't be offended, but I was scared of you at first. You have to admit you do a funny sort of job!'

'Don't worry about it.'

'And I was scared of Monsieur Marechall too. You don't often come across people in his line of work either!'

'Thank goodness for people like him, though! Rats and rodents do all kinds of damage ...'

'Rats! Right, yes, of course ... Anyway, he's quite harmless now.'

'I'm worried about him. If you'd seen him earlier ... I really thought he ...'

'Now now, Rose, don't cry. The docs can work miracles these days.'

'Let's hope so, oh, let's ... I'm sorry, it's just this is the first time for me!'

'For what?'

'Well, love at first sight, just like in books! At my age, it's hardly likely to happen again!'

'Now come on, he's not dead, he's just old ... Look! Here he comes now, with Bernard.'

Rose rushed to the window, half smothering Violette between her breasts.

'He really shouldn't be walking about like that after what he put me through today. It's not right ...'

Bernard was shuttling the milk carton from one hand to the other, trying to appear composed, while slowing his steps to keep pace with Simon. He was sure he was going to come out with something stupid, but faced with Monsieur Marechall's inscrutable silence, he bit the bullet and blurted out, 'Monsieur Marechall, I wanted to say—'

'Don't say anything.'

'OK, I won't. But you can still count on me. I'll finish the job, just like I said.'

'We're leaving tomorrow. You and me, that's it.'

'OK, Monsieur Marechall, OK. It's just I thought that Fiona and—'

'Just you and me!'

Monsieur Marechall had stopped walking and was clutching Bernard's arm with more strength than he looked capable of: an eagle's grip. Despite his frail state, with the wind ruffling his tufts of white goose-down hair, there was still a glint of steely determination in his eyes.

'Tomorrow, you'll take me back to the hotel in Vals, and you'll do exactly as I say, from start to finish. After that ... do what you want, I don't care.'

Simon let go of his arm and started walking again, slowly placing one foot in front of the other, head bowed, shoulders hunched.

Anaïs had spent the day eating and drinking, drinking and eating, until she made herself sick. Then, after vomiting, she started all over again, mixing cassoulet, chocolate and sardines on the same plate. Strictly speaking, all the supplies she had bought that morning were supposed to keep her going through the afterlife, but since Anaïs felt that journey might be a bit on the long side, she told herself that by devouring the lot in record time, eternity would somehow be speeded up. The logic of this was debatable, but there must have been something to it, because several hours had passed without her noticing. It was dark outside.

'Shit, eleven o'clock already! What shall I have for supper? Soup!'

The little creatures thought this a splendid idea, clapping with both hands (and sometimes even more hands than that, as some of the little monsters had four or even six of them). A nice soup for dinner, an eleven o'clock broth.

Soup is a universal dish, eaten everywhere in the world. All you need is water and anything else you can find to chuck in.

The first bottle of Negrita was empty, of course. The liquid in the second bottle came up to the chin of the woman on the label or, turned upside down, to the level of her madras cotton turban. Anaïs tipped it back and forth several times, pondering the passing of time the way others do with an hourglass. There was no question: time definitely went by more quickly in liquid form. Anaïs poured herself a glass to celebrate her astute observation. She could have been a researcher, a great scientist like Marie Curie, with a bit of help. But no one ever had helped her. What a waste! Only the people who discovered things got rewarded for it, but, hell, you had to look for things before discovering them! The fact that liquid time passed more quickly than mineral time, that was quite a revelation, wasn't it? ... Well, it was their loss. She would keep that one to herself and it would be centuries before they understood this irrefutable natural law for themselves.

The kitchen had gradually started to look like an upturned dustbin again. The spiders were spinning webs in the corners once more; the grease-coated lino was slippery underfoot just like in the good old days, and the fluff balls had gathered again like sheep quietly grazing along the skirting boards.

'So what? You don't care about me; well, I don't care about you either.'

Standing with her legs wide apart, wobbling on her rocker soles, Anaïs filled a big stockpot with water and threw in a handful of pasta, another of rice, a tin of peas, a packet of lardons, a sprinkling of grated Gruyère, a few tears ...

'He could at least have sent me a postcard. A stupid sunset or something ...'

The little creatures moaned along with her. Anaïs chased them off with a whack of the tea towel.

'Get the hell out of here! Can't you see you're getting on my nerves? You're always under my feet! ... Now where on earth have I put the matches?'

She could not see clearly, or else she saw too clearly, as though looking through a magnifying glass. Every object appeared ridiculously large. Failing to judge distances, she kept knocking things over like skittles, until in the end she no longer dared touch anything and stood, panting and puffing like a whale, both hands flat on the table. A whistling sound came out of nowhere, boring into her eardrums, while a sickening smell turned her stomach and dulled her mind. She sank to her knees, bringing with her the oilcloth and everything on top of it.

'What a godawful mess ...'

She slumped forward, flat on her face. The life drained out of her body like oil from a drum.

'Do you think you will actually visit Rose in Belgium?'

He did not respond.

'She'll be waiting for you.'

'Better to be waiting for someone than for nothing at all.'

'The reason I'm asking is I really like Rose. I'm glad she gets on well with Fiona and Violette. It means they're not on their own any more. It's like we're a little family.'

'Will you stop going on about your "little family"?'

'Ah, come on, you say that but what about you and Rose?'

'Would you mind your own business? You'll see your girls again in two days. In the meantime, just let it drop, OK?'

'All right, Monsieur Marechall, I won't mention them again. It's just that when you're happy you want to shout about it, don't you?'

Simon refrained from making a snide comment. There was no point. Bernard wore his new-found happiness like a shining suit of armour. The stupid fool couldn't help smiling at everything: the other cars cutting him up; the leaden sky just waiting for a sign before erupting; the dingy, humdrum buildings that lined the road; the police cars lying in wait behind the plane trees. Simon could almost hear the needles clicking away inside his head, knitting together a bright little future with a little job, a little house, a little wife, a little daughter ...

'Will you stop thinking!'

'I'm not thinking, Monsieur Marechall, I'm watching the road. Drat, there are road works; there'll be traffic jams. Here comes the rain!'

Flashing signs forced the cars to slow down and get into one lane. The windscreen wipers swept the raindrops away, leaving fleeting fan shapes on the glass. Only one thing threatened to mar Bernard's constant bliss, which was the task Simon planned to entrust him with. The slowing of the traffic seemed like an invitation to test the water.

'What will you do after you go back to Fiona and the baby?'

'We're heading back up to Bron. My hand's almost better so I can go back to my job. We'll just have to find a bigger flat because my bedsit ... Well, when you put the key in the door you pretty much break the window, if you see what I mean. Rents are steep in town, but we'll manage somehow. Fiona's smart, she'll find herself a little job.'

'A little job, a little flat! Never been tempted to think big?'

'Very funny ... We get by as best we can! I wasn't born with a silver spoon in my mouth. You've seen my mother ... I need to look after her as well. It won't be easy, but love gives you strength. And the other half of my pay from you will be a good start.'

'You won't get very far with that.'

'As far as Bron. Don't you worry, I only lost two fingers, I've still got both arms!'

And he smiled, just as he had when Simon first met him on the bench and he had said: 'It's only my little finger and fourth finger. I never used them.' The kid had a talent for survival, like newborn babies found alive in dustbins.

'Listen, Bernard. Apart from yesterday's escapade, which we'll pass over, I've been very pleased with you. You've always delivered, even in, shall we say ... "delicate" situations. So if you wanted—'

'No, Monsieur Marechall, I'll have to say no straight out. I like you very much, but your job, well, it's just not for me. I'm sure it pays well, and maybe I'm just a pathetic person with pathetic dreams, but at least I can look at myself in the mirror every morning and not feel ashamed. I'm not criticising you, I know deep down you're not such a bad person, but I don't want to end up sad and lonely like you. Each to his own, Monsieur Marechall, each to his own.'

'Hang on a minute, I'm not offering you a job! I was about to ask a favour.'

'Oh. What kind of favour?'

'The kind of favour you can only ask of a friend.'

The little Playmobile people were waving flags to direct the traffic. The cars gradually got back up to cruising speed.

They arrived in Vals-les-Bains late in the afternoon. It was still raining, not heavily, but persistently. Bernard found a parking space right outside the Grand Hôtel de Lyon. He was not smiling now. He kept his hands on the wheel and stared straight ahead.

'OK, Bernard, so eight o'clock tomorrow morning? Right, Bernard?'

'Yes! Eight o'clock tomorrow morning. You really are messed-up though, Monsieur Marechall.'

'Let's shake hands.'

Before getting out of the car, they both noticed the child seat still strapped to the back seat. Simon shook his head, smiling.

'Handy, those things.'

They parted on the pavement, one stepping into the hotel lobby, the other heading towards the old town. Neither looked back.

Editions Gallic returns to Gallic Books' original mission of bringing together the very best of French in English. A combination of classic and contemporary French literature, the collection aims to bring readers back to old favourites as well as introducing new titles from iconic francophone authors.

Also available from Editions Gallic:

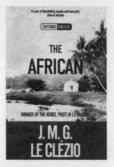

The African
J. M. G. Le Clézio
Translated by C. Dickson

'A work of bewitching beauty and humanity'
Chinua Achebe

In 1948, a young J. M. G. Le Clézio left behind a still-devastated Europe with his mother and brother to join his father, a military doctor in Nigeria, from whom he had been separated by the war. In his characteristically intimate, poetic voice, the Nobel Prize-winning author relates both the child's dazzled discovery of freedom in the African savannah and the torment of recalling his fractured relationship with a rigid, authoritarian father.

The African is a memoir of a lost childhood and a tribute to a father whom Le Clézio never really knew. His legacy is the passionate anti-colonialism that the author has carried through his life.

ISBN: 9781910477854
e-ISBN: 9781910477892

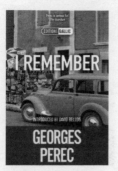

I Remember
Georges Perec
Translated by Philip Terry

'Perec is a great storyteller and a wry humorist'
The Telegraph

Both an affectionate portrait of mid-century Paris and a daring memoir, Georges Perec's *I Remember* is available in English in the UK for the first time, with an introduction by David Bellos.

In 480 numbered statements, all beginning identically with 'I remember', Perec records a stream of individual memories of a childhood in post-war France, while posing wider questions about memory and nostalgia.

As playful and puzzling as the best of his novels, *I Remember* is an ode to life: the ordinary, the extraordinary, and the sometimes trivial, as seen through the eyes of the irreplaceable Georges Perec.

ISBN: 9781910477854
e-ISBN: 9781910477892